NINE
OF
HARTE'S

SHORT STORIES
OF THE OLD WEST

BRET
HARTE

BLACKBIRD BOOKS
NEW YORK • LOS ANGELES

A Blackbird Classic, December 2020

Manufactured in the United States of America.

The events and characters depicted in this book are
fictional.

Cataloging-in-Publication Data

Harte, Bret.
Nine of Harte's / Bret Harte.
p. cm.
1. Western stories. 2. West (U.S.)—Fiction.
3. Frontier and pioneer life—West (U.S.)—Fiction.
4. California—Social life and customs—Fiction I. Title.
PS1829 .N56 2020 813′.4—dc23 2020950991

Blackbird Books
www.bbirdbooks.com
email us at editor@bbirdbooks.com

ISBN 978-1-61053-044-6

First Blackbird Edition

10 9 8 7 6 5 4 3 2 1

CONTENTS

NINE
OF
HARTE'S

THE LUCK OF ROARING CAMP

There was commotion in Roaring Camp. It could not have been a fight, for in 1850 that was not novel enough to have called together the entire settlement. The ditches and claims were not only deserted, but Tuttle's grocery had contributed its gamblers, who, it will be remembered, calmly continued their game the day that French Pete and Kanaka Joe shot each other to death over the bar in the front room. The whole camp was collected before a rude cabin on the outer edge of the clearing. Conversation was carried on in a low tone, but the name of a woman was frequently repeated. It was a name familiar enough in the camp—Cherokee Sal.

Perhaps the less said of her the better. She was a coarse and, it is to be feared, a very sinful woman. But at that time she was the only woman in Roaring Camp, and was just then lying in sore extremity, when she most needed the ministration of her own sex. Dissolute, abandoned, and irreclaimable, she was yet suffering a martyrdom hard enough to bear even when veiled by sympathizing womanhood, but now terrible in her loneliness. The primal curse had come to her in that original isolation which must have made the punishment of the first transgression so dreadful. It was, perhaps, part of the expiation of her sin that, at a moment when she most lacked her sex's intuitive tenderness and care, she met only the half-contemptuous faces of her masculine associates. Yet a few of the spectators were, I think, touched by her sufferings. Sandy Tipton thought it was rough on Sal, and, in the contemplation of her condition, for a moment rose superior to the fact that he had an ace and two bowers in his sleeve.

It will be seen also that the situation was novel. Deaths were by no means uncommon in Roaring Camp, but a birth was a new thing. People had been dismissed the camp effectively, finally, and with no possibility of return; but this was the first time that anybody had been introduced *ab initio*. Hence the excitement.

"You go in there, Stumpy," said a prominent citizen known as Kentuck, addressing one of the loungers. "Go in there, and see what you kin do. You've had experience in them things."

Perhaps there was a fitness in the selection. Stumpy, in other climes, had been the putative head of two families; in fact, it was owing to some legal informality in these proceedings that Roaring Camp—a city of refuge—was indebted to his company. The crowd approved the choice, and Stumpy was wise enough to bow to the majority. The door closed on the extempore surgeon and midwife, and Roaring Camp sat down outside, smoked its pipe, and awaited the issue.

The assemblage numbered about a hundred men. One or two of these were actual fugitives from justice, some were criminal, and all were reckless. Physically they exhibited no indication of their past lives and character. The greatest scamp had a Raphael face, with a profusion of blonde hair; Oakhurst, a gambler, had the melancholy air and intellectual abstraction of a Hamlet; the coolest and most courageous man was scarcely over five feet in height, with a soft voice and an embarrassed, timid manner. The term "roughs" applied to them was a distinction rather than a definition. Perhaps in the minor details of fingers, toes, ears, etc., the camp may have been deficient, but these slight omissions did not detract from their aggregate force. The strongest man had but three fingers on his right hand; the best shot had but one eye.

Such was the physical aspect of the men that were dispersed around the cabin. The camp lay in a triangular valley between two hills and a river. The only outlet was a steep trail over the summit of a hill that faced the cabin, now illuminated by the rising moon. The suffering woman might have seen it from the rude bunk whereon she lay—seen it winding like a silver thread until it was lost in the stars above.

A fire of withered pine boughs added sociability to the gathering. By degrees, the natural levity of Roaring Camp returned. Bets were freely offered and taken regarding the result. Three to five that "Sal would get through with it;" even that the child would survive; side bets as to the sex and complexion of the coming stranger. In the midst of an excited discussion an exclamation came from those nearest the door, and the camp stopped to listen. Above the swaying and moaning of the pines, the swift rush of the river, and the crackling of the fire rose a sharp, querulous cry, a cry unlike anything heard before in the camp. The pines stopped moaning, the river ceased to rush, and the fire to crackle. It seemed as if Nature had stopped to listen too.

The camp rose to its feet as one man! It was proposed to explode a barrel of gunpowder; but in consideration of the situation of the mother, better counsels prevailed, and only a few revolvers were discharged; for whether owing to the rude surgery of the camp, or some other reason, Cherokee Sal was sinking fast. Within an hour, she had climbed, as it were, that rugged road that led to the stars, and so passed out of Roaring Camp, its sin and shame, forever. I do not think that the announcement disturbed them much, except in speculation as to the fate of the child. "Can he live now?" was asked of Stumpy. The answer was doubtful. The only other being of Cherokee Sal's sex and maternal condition in the settlement was an ass. There was some conjecture as to fitness, but the experiment was tried. It was less problematical than the ancient treatment of Romulus and Remus, and apparently as successful.

When these details were completed, which exhausted another hour, the door was opened, and the anxious crowd of men, who had already formed themselves into a queue, entered in single file. Beside the low bunk or shelf, on which the figure of the mother was starkly outlined below the blankets, stood a pine table. On this a candle box was placed, and within it, swathed in staring red flannel, lay the last arrival at Roaring Camp. Beside the candle box was placed a hat. Its use was soon indicated. "Gentlemen," said Stumpy, with a singular mixture of authority and *ex officio* complacency, "gentlemen will please pass in at the front door, round the table, and out at the back door. Them as wishes to contribute anything toward the orphan will find a hat handy." The first man entered with his hat on; he uncovered, however, as he looked about him, and so unconsciously set an example to the next. In such communities good and bad actions are catching. As the procession filed in, comments were audible—criticisms addressed perhaps rather to Stumpy in the character of showman: "Is that him?" "Mighty small specimen;" "Hasn't more'n got the color;" "Ain't bigger nor a derringer." The contributions were as characteristic: A silver tobacco box; a doubloon; a navy revolver, silver mounted; a gold specimen; a very beautifully embroidered lady's handkerchief (from Oakhurst the gambler); a diamond breastpin; a diamond ring (suggested by the pin, with the remark from the giver that he "saw that pin and went two diamonds better"); a slung-shot; a Bible (contributor not detected); a golden spur; a silver teaspoon (the initials, I regret to say, were not the giver's); a pair of surgeon's shears; a lancet; a Bank of England note for £5; and about $200 in loose gold and silver coin. During these proceedings Stumpy maintained a silence as impassive as the dead on his left, a gravity as inscrutable as that of the newly born on his right. Only one incident occurred to break the monotony of the curious procession. As Kentuck bent over the candle box half curiously, the child turned, and, in a spasm of pain, caught at his groping finger, and held it fast for a moment. Kentuck looked foolish and embarrassed. Something like a blush tried to assert itself in his weather-beaten cheek. "The d—d little cuss!" he said, as he extricated his finger, with perhaps more tenderness and care than he might have been deemed capable of showing. He held that finger a little apart from its fellows as he went out, and examined it curiously. The examination provoked the same original remark in regard to the child. In fact, he seemed to enjoy repeating it. "He rastled with my finger," he remarked to Tipton, holding up the member, "the d—d little cuss!"

It was four o'clock before the camp sought repose. A light burnt in the cabin where the watchers sat, for Stumpy did not go to bed that night. Nor did Kentuck. He drank quite freely, and related with great gusto his experience, invariably ending with his characteristic condemnation of the newcomer. It seemed to relieve him of any unjust implication of sentiment, and Kentuck had the weaknesses of the nobler sex. When everybody else had gone to bed, he walked down to the river and whistled reflectingly. Then he walked up the gulch past the cabin, still whistling with demonstrative unconcern. At a large redwood tree he paused and retraced his steps, and again passed the cabin. Halfway down to the river's bank he again paused, and then returned and knocked at the door. It was opened by Stumpy. "How goes it?" said Kentuck, looking past Stumpy toward the candle box. "All serene!" replied Stumpy. "Anything up?" "Nothing." There was a pause—an embarrassing one—Stumpy still holding the door. Then Kentuck had recourse to his finger, which he held up to Stumpy. "Rastled with it—the d—d little cuss," he said, and retired.

The next day Cherokee Sal had such rude sepulture as Roaring Camp afforded. After her body had been committed to the hillside, there was a formal meeting of the camp to discuss what should be done with her infant. A resolution to adopt it was unanimous and enthusiastic. But an animated discussion in regard to the manner and feasibility of providing for its wants at once sprang up. It was remarkable that the argument partook of none of those fierce personalities with which discussions were usually conducted at Roaring Camp. Tipton proposed that they should send the child to Red Dog—a distance of forty miles—where female attention could be procured. But the unlucky suggestion met with fierce and unanimous opposition. It was evident that no plan which entailed parting from their new acquisition would for a moment be entertained. "Besides," said Tom Ryder, "them fellows at

Red Dog would swap it, and ring in somebody else on us." A disbelief in the honesty of other camps prevailed at Roaring Camp, as in other places.

The introduction of a female nurse in the camp also met with objection. It was argued that no decent woman could be prevailed to accept Roaring Camp as her home, and the speaker urged that "they didn't want any more of the other kind." This unkind allusion to the defunct mother, harsh as it may seem, was the first spasm of propriety, the first symptom of the camp's regeneration. Stumpy advanced nothing. Perhaps he felt a certain delicacy in interfering with the selection of a possible successor in office. But when questioned, he averred stoutly that he and Jinny—the mammal before alluded to—could manage to rear the child. There was something original, independent, and heroic about the plan that pleased the camp. Stumpy was retained. Certain articles were sent for to Sacramento. "Mind," said the treasurer, as he pressed a bag of gold dust into the expressman's hand, "the best that can be got—lace, you know, and filigree work and frills— d—n the cost!"

Strange to say, the child thrived. Perhaps the invigorating climate of the mountain camp was compensation for material deficiencies. Nature took the foundling to her broader breast. In that rare atmosphere of the Sierra foothills—that air pungent with balsamic odor, that ethereal cordial at once bracing and exhilarating—he may have found food and nourishment, or a subtle chemistry that transmuted ass's milk to lime and phosphorus. Stumpy inclined to the belief that it was the latter and good nursing. "Me and that ass," he would say, "has been father and mother to him! Don't you," he would add, apostrophizing the helpless bundle before him, "never go back on us."

By the time he was a month old the necessity of giving him a name became apparent. He had generally been known as "The Kid," "Stumpy's Boy," "The Coyote" (an allusion to his vocal powers), and even by Kentuck's endearing diminutive of "The d—d little cuss." But these were felt to be vague and unsatisfactory, and were at last dismissed under another influence. Gamblers and adventurers are generally superstitious, and Oakhurst one day declared that the baby had brought "the luck" to Roaring Camp. It was certain that of late they had been successful. "Luck" was the name agreed upon, with the prefix of Tommy for greater convenience. No allusion was made to the mother, and the father was unknown. "It's better," said the philosophical Oakhurst, "to take a fresh deal all round. Call him Luck, and start him fair." A day was accordingly set apart for the christening. What was meant by this ceremony the reader may imagine who has already gathered some idea of the reckless irreverence of Roaring Camp. The master of ceremonies was one "Boston," a noted wag, and the occasion seemed to promise the greatest facetiousness. This ingenious satirist had spent two days in preparing a burlesque of the Church service, with pointed local allusions. The choir was properly trained, and Sandy Tipton was to stand godfather. But after the procession had marched to the grove with music and banners, and the child had been deposited before a mock altar, Stumpy stepped before the expectant crowd. "It ain't my style to spoil fun, boys," said the little man, stoutly eying the faces around him, "but it strikes me that this thing ain't exactly on the squar. It's playing it pretty low down on this yer baby to ring in fun on him that he ain't goin' to understand. And ef there's goin' to be any godfathers round, I'd like to see who's got any better rights than me." A silence followed Stumpy's speech. To the credit of all humorists be it said that the first man to acknowledge its justice was the satirist thus stopped of his fun. "But," said Stumpy, quickly following up his advantage, "we're here for a christening, and we'll have it. I proclaim you Thomas Luck, according to the laws of the United States and the State of California, so help me God." It was the first time that the name of the Deity had been otherwise uttered than profanely in the camp. The form of christening was perhaps even more ludicrous than the satirist had conceived; but strangely enough, nobody saw it and nobody laughed. Tommy was christened as seriously as he would have been under a Christian roof, and cried and was comforted in as orthodox fashion.

And so the work of regeneration began in Roaring Camp. Almost imperceptibly a change came over the settlement. The cabin assigned to Tommy Luck—or The Luck, as he was more frequently called—first showed signs of improvement. It was kept scrupulously clean and whitewashed. Then it was boarded, clothed, and papered. The rosewood, cradle, packed eighty miles by mule, had, in Stumpy's way of putting it, "sorter killed the rest of the furniture." So the rehabilitation of the cabin became a necessity. The men who were in the habit of lounging in at Stumpy's to see how The Luck got on seemed to appreciate the change, and in self-defense the rival establishment of Tuttle's grocery bestirred itself and imported a carpet and mirrors. The reflections of the latter on the appearance of Roaring Camp tended to produce stricter habits of personal cleanliness. Again Stumpy imposed a kind of quarantine upon those who aspired to the honor and privilege of holding The Luck. It was a cruel mortification to Kentuck—who, in the carelessness of a large nature and the habits of frontier life, had begun to regard all garments as a second cuticle, which, like a snake's, only sloughed off through decay—to be debarred this privilege from certain prudential reasons. Yet such was the subtle influence of innovation that he thereafter appeared regularly every afternoon in a clean shirt and face still shining from his ablutions. Nor were moral and social sanitary laws neglected. Tommy, who was supposed to spend his whole existence in a persistent attempt to repose, must not be disturbed by noise. The shouting and yelling, which had gained the camp its infelicitous title, were not permitted within hearing distance of Stumpy's. The men conversed in whispers or smoked with Indian gravity. Profanity was tacitly given up in these sacred precincts, and throughout the camp a popular form of expletive, known as "D—n the luck!" and "Curse the luck!" was abandoned, as having a new personal bearing. Vocal music was not interdicted, being supposed to have a soothing, tranquilizing quality; and one song, sung by "Man-o'-War Jack," an English sailor from her Majesty's Australian colonies, was quite popular as a lullaby. It was a lugubrious recital of the exploits of "the Arethusa, Seventy-four," in a muffled minor, ending with a prolonged dying fall at the burden of each verse," On b-oo-o-ard of the Arethusa." It was a fine sight to see Jack holding The Luck, rocking from side to side as if with the motion of a ship, and crooning forth this naval ditty. Either through the peculiar rocking of Jack or the length of his song—it contained ninety stanzas, and was continued with conscientious deliberation to the bitter end—the lullaby generally had the desired effect. At such times the men would lie at full length under the trees in the soft summer twilight, smoking their pipes and drinking in the melodious utterances. An indistinct idea that this was pastoral happiness pervaded the camp. "This 'ere kind o' think," said the Cockney Simmons, meditatively reclining on his elbow, "is 'evingly." It reminded him of Greenwich.

On the long summer days The Luck was usually carried to the gulch from whence the golden store of Roaring Camp was taken. There, on a blanket spread over pine boughs, he would lie while the men were working in the ditches below. Latterly there was a rude attempt to decorate this bower with flowers and sweet-smelling shrubs, and generally someone would bring him a cluster of wild honeysuckles, azaleas, or the painted blossoms of Las Mariposas. The men had suddenly awakened to the fact that there were beauty and significance in these trifles, which they had so long trodden carelessly beneath their feet. A flake of glittering mica, a fragment of variegated quartz, a bright pebble from the bed of the creek, became beautiful to eyes thus cleared and strengthened, and were invariably put aside for The Luck. It was wonderful how many treasures the woods and hillsides yielded that "would do for Tommy." Surrounded by playthings such as never child out of fairyland had before, it is to be hoped that Tommy was content. He appeared to be serenely happy, albeit there was an infantine gravity about him, a contemplative light in his round gray eyes, that sometimes worried Stumpy. He was always tractable and quiet, and it is recorded that once, having crept beyond his "corral"—a hedge of tessellated pine boughs, which surrounded his bed—he dropped over the bank on his head in the soft earth, and remained with his mottled legs in the air in that position for at least five minutes with unflinching gravity. He was extricated without a murmur. I hesitate to record the many other instances of his sagacity, which rest, unfortunately, upon the statements of prejudiced friends. Some of them were not without a tinge of superstition. "I crep' up the bank just now," said Kentuck one day, in a breathless state of excitement, "and dern my skin if he wasn't a-talking to a jaybird as was a-sittin' on his lap. There they was, just as free and sociable as any-

17

thing you please, a-jawin' at each other just like two cherrybums." Howbeit, whether creeping over the pine boughs or lying lazily on his back blinking at the leaves above him, to him the birds sang, the squirrels chattered, and the flowers bloomed. Nature was his nurse and playfellow. For him she would let slip between the leaves golden shafts of sunlight that fell just within his grasp; she would send wandering breezes to visit him with the balm of bay and resinous gum; to him the tall redwoods nodded familiarly and sleepily, the bumblebees buzzed, and the rooks cawed a slumberous accompaniment.

Such was the golden summer of Roaring Camp. They were "flush times," and the luck was with them. The claims had yielded enormously. The camp was jealous of its privileges and looked suspiciously on strangers. No encouragement was given to immigration, and, to make their seclusion more perfect, the land on either side of the mountain wall that surrounded the camp they duly preempted. This, and a reputation for singular proficiency with the revolver, kept the reserve of Roaring Camp inviolate. The expressman—their only connecting link with the surrounding world—sometimes told wonderful stories of the camp. He would say, "They've a street up there in Roaring that would lay over any street in Red Dog.

They've got vines and flowers round their houses, and they wash themselves twice a day. But they're mighty rough on strangers, and they worship an Ingin baby."

With the prosperity of the camp came a desire for further improvement. It was proposed to build a hotel in the following spring, and to invite one or two decent families to reside there for the sake of The Luck, who might perhaps profit by female companionship. The sacrifice that this concession to the sex cost these men, who were fiercely skeptical in regard to its general virtue and usefulness, can only be accounted for by their affection for Tommy. A few still held out. But the resolve could not be carried into effect for three months, and the minority meekly yielded in the hope that something might turn up to prevent it. And it did.

The winter of 1851 will long be remembered in the foothills. The snow lay deep on the Sierras, and every mountain creek became a river, and every river a lake. Each gorge and gulch was transformed into a tumultuous watercourse that descended the hillsides, tearing down giant trees and scattering its drift and debris along the plain. Red Dog had been twice under water, and Roaring Camp had been forewarned. "Water put the gold into them gulches," said Stumpy. "It's been here once and will be here again!" And that night the North Fork suddenly leaped over its banks and swept up the triangular valley of Roaring Camp.

In the confusion of rushing water, crashing trees, and crackling timber, and the darkness which seemed to flow with the water and blot out the fair valley, but little could be done to collect the scattered camp. When the morning broke, the cabin of Stumpy, nearest the river- bank, was gone. Higher up the gulch they found the body of its unlucky owner; but the pride, the hope, the joy, The Luck, of Roaring Camp had disappeared. They were returning with sad hearts when a shout from the bank recalled them.

It was a relief boat from down the river. They had picked up, they said, a man and an infant, nearly exhausted, about two miles below. Did anybody know them, and did they belong here?

It needed but a glance to show them Kentuck lying there, cruelly crushed and bruised, but still holding The Luck of Roaring Camp in his arms. As they bent over the strangely assorted pair, they saw that the child was cold and pulseless. "He is dead," said one. Kentuck opened his eyes. "Dead?" he repeated feebly. "Yes, my man, and you are dying too." A smile lit the eyes of the expiring Kentuck. "Dying!" he repeated; "he's a-taking me with him. Tell the boys I've got The Luck with me now;" and the strong man, clinging to the frail babe as a drowning man is said to cling to a straw, drifted away into the shadowy river that flows forever to the unknown sea.

THE OUTCASTS OF POKER FLAT

As Mr. John Oakhurst, gambler, stepped into the main street of Poker Flat on the morning of the 23rd of November, 1850, he was conscious of a change in its moral atmosphere since the preceding night. Two or three men, conversing earnestly together, ceased as he approached, and exchanged significant glances. There was a Sabbath lull in the air, which, in a settlement unused to Sabbath influences, looked ominous.

Mr. Oakhurst's calm, handsome face betrayed small concern in these indications. Whether he was conscious of any predisposing cause was another question. "I reckon they're after somebody," he reflected; "likely it's me." He returned to his pocket the handkerchief with which he had been whipping away the red dust of Poker Flat from his neat boots, and quietly discharged his mind of any further conjecture.

In point of fact, Poker Flat was after somebody. It had lately suffered the loss of several thousand dollars, two valuable horses, and a prominent citizen. It was experiencing a spasm of virtuous reaction, quite as lawless and ungovernable as any of the acts that had provoked it. A secret committee had determined to rid the town of all improper persons. This was done permanently in regard of two men who were then hanging from the boughs of a sycamore in the gulch, and temporarily in the banishment of certain other objectionable characters. I regret to say that some of these were ladies. It is but due to the sex, however, to state that their impropriety was professional, and it was only in such easily established standards of evil that Poker Flat ventured to sit in judgment.

Mr. Oakhurst was right in supposing that he was included in this category. A few of the committee had urged hanging him as a possible example and a sure method of reimbursing themselves from his pockets of the sums he had won from them. "It's agin justice," said Jim Wheeler, "to let this yer young man from Roaring Camp—an entire stranger—carry away our money." But a crude sentiment of equity residing in the breasts of those who had been fortunate enough to win from Mr. Oakhurst overruled this narrower local prejudice.

Mr. Oakhurst received his sentence with philosophic calmness, nonetheless coolly that he was aware of the hesitation of his judges. He was too much of a gambler not to accept fate. With him, life was at best an uncertain game, and he recognized the usual percentage in favor of the dealer.

A body of armed men accompanied the deported wickedness of Poker Flat to the outskirts of the settlement. Besides Mr. Oakhurst, who was known to be a coolly desperate man, and for whose intimidation the armed escort was intended, the expatriated party consisted of a young woman familiarly known as "The Duchess;" another who had won the title of "Mother Shipton;" and "Uncle Billy," a suspected, sluice robber and confirmed drunkard. The cavalcade provoked no comments from the spectators, nor was any word uttered by the escort. Only when the gulch which marked the uttermost limit of Poker Flat was reached, the leader spoke briefly and to the point. The exiles were forbidden to return at the peril of their lives.

As the escort disappeared, their pent-up feelings found vent in a few hysterical tears from the Duchess, some bad language from Mother Shipton, and a Parthian volley of expletives from Uncle Billy. The philosophic Oakhurst alone remained silent. He listened calmly to Mother Shipton's desire to cut somebody's heart out, to the repeated statements of the Duchess that she would die in the road, and to the alarming oaths that seemed to be bumped out of Uncle Billy as he rode forward. With the easy good humor characteristic of his class, he insisted upon exchanging his own riding-horse, Five-Spot, for the sorry mule which the Duchess rode. But even this act did not draw the party into any closer sympathy. The young woman readjusted her somewhat draggled plumes with a feeble, faded coquetry; Mother Shipton eyed the possessor of Five-Spot with malevolence, and Uncle Billy included the whole party in one sweeping anathema.

The road to Sandy Bar—a camp that, not having as yet experienced the regenerating influences of Poker Flat, consequently seemed to offer some invitation to the emigrants—lay over a steep mountain range. It was distant a day's severe travel. In that advanced season the party soon passed out of the moist, temperate regions of the foothills into the dry, cold, bracing air of the Sierras. The trail was narrow and difficult. At noon the Duchess, rolling out of her saddle upon the ground, declared her intention of going no farther, and the party halted.

The spot was singularly wild and impressive. A wooded amphitheater, surrounded on three sides by precipitous cliffs of naked granite, sloped gently toward the crest of another precipice that overlooked the valley. It was, undoubtedly, the most suitable spot for a camp, had camping been advisable. But Mr. Oakhurst knew that scarcely half the journey to Sandy Bar was accomplished, and the party were not equipped or provisioned for delay. This fact he pointed out to his companions curtly, with a philosophic commentary on the folly of "throwing up their hand before the game was played out." But they were furnished with liquor, which in this emergency stood them in place of food, fuel, rest, and prescience. In spite of his remonstrances, it was not long before they were more or less under its influence. Uncle Billy passed rapidly from a bellicose state into one of stupor, the Duchess became maudlin, and Mother Shipton snored. Mr. Oakhurst alone remained erect, leaning against a rock, calmly surveying them.

Mr. Oakhurst did not drink. It interfered with a profession which required coolness, impassiveness, and presence of mind, and, in his own language, he "couldn't afford it." As he gazed at his recumbent fellow exiles, the loneliness begotten of his pariah trade, his habits of life, his very vices, for the first time seriously oppressed him. He bestirred himself in dusting his black clothes, washing his hands and face, and other acts characteristic of his studiously neat habits, and for a moment forgot his annoyance. The thought of deserting his weaker and more pitiable companions never perhaps occurred to him. Yet he could not help feeling the want of that excitement which, singularly enough, was most conducive to that calm equanimity for which he was notorious. He looked at the gloomy walls that rose a thousand feet sheer above the circling pines around him, at the sky ominously clouded, at the valley below, already deepening into shadow; and, doing so, suddenly he heard his own name called.

A horseman slowly ascended the trail. In the fresh, open face of the newcomer Mr. Oakhurst recognized Tom Simson, otherwise known as "The Innocent," of Sandy Bar. He had met him some months before over a "little game," and had, with perfect equanimity, won the entire fortune—amounting to some forty dollars—of that guileless youth. After the game was finished, Mr. Oakhurst drew the youthful speculator behind the door and thus addressed him: "Tommy, you're a good little man, but you can't gamble worth a cent. Don't try it over again." He then handed him his money back, pushed him gently from the room, and so made a devoted slave of Tom Simson.

There was a remembrance of this in his boyish and enthusiastic greeting of Mr. Oakhurst. He had started, he said, to go to Poker Flat to seek his fortune. "Alone?" No, not exactly alone; in fact (a giggle), he had run away with Piney Woods. Didn't Mr. Oakhurst remember Piney? She that used to wait on the table at the Temperance House? They had been engaged a long time, but old Jake Woods had objected, and so they had run away, and were going to Poker Flat to be married, and here they were. And they were tired out, and how lucky it was they had found a place to camp, and company. All this the Innocent delivered rapidly, while Piney, a stout, comely damsel of fifteen, emerged from behind the pine tree, where she had been blushing unseen, and rode to the side of her lover.

Mr. Oakhurst seldom troubled himself with sentiment, still less with propriety; but he had a vague idea that the situation was not fortunate. He retained, however, his presence of mind sufficiently to kick Uncle Billy, who was about to say something, and Uncle Billy was sober enough to recognize in Mr. Oakhurst's kick a superior power that would not bear trifling. He then endeavored to dissuade Tom Simson from delaying further, but in vain. He even pointed out the fact that there was no provision, nor means of making a camp. But, unluckily, the Innocent met this objection by assuring the party that he was provided with an extra mule loaded with provisions, and by the discovery of a rude attempt at a log house near the trail. "Piney can stay with Mrs. Oakhurst," said the Innocent, pointing to the Duchess, "and I can shift for myself."

Nothing but Mr. Oakhurst's admonishing foot saved Uncle Billy from bursting into a roar of laughter. As it was, he felt compelled to retire up the canyon until he could recover his gravity. There he confided the joke to the tall pine trees, with many slaps of his leg, contortions of his face, and the usual profanity. But when he returned to the party, he found them seated by a fire—for the air had grown strangely chill and the sky overcast—in apparently amicable conversation. Piney was actually talking in an impulsive girlish fashion to the Duchess, who was listening with an interest and animation she had not shown for many days. The Innocent was holding forth, apparently with equal effect, to Mr. Oakhurst and Mother Shipton, who was actually relaxing into amiability. "Is this yer a d—d picnic?" said Uncle Billy, with inward scorn, as he surveyed the sylvan group, the glancing firelight, and the tethered animals in the foreground. Suddenly an idea mingled with the alcoholic fumes that disturbed his brain. It was apparently of a jocular nature, for he felt impelled to slap his leg again and cram his fist into his mouth.

As the shadows crept slowly up the mountain, a slight breeze rocked the tops of the pine trees and moaned through their long and gloomy aisles. The ruined cabin, patched and covered with pine boughs, was set apart for the ladies. As the lovers parted, they unaffectedly exchanged a kiss, so honest and sincere that it might have been heard above the swaying pines. The frail Duchess and the malevolent Mother Shipton were probably too stunned to remark upon this last evidence of simplicity, and so turned without a word to the hut. The fire was replenished, the men lay down before the door, and in a few minutes were asleep.

Mr. Oakhurst was a light sleeper. Toward morning he awoke benumbed and cold. As he stirred the dying fire, the wind, which was now blowing strongly, brought to his cheek that which caused the blood to leave it—snow!

He started to his feet with the intention of awakening the sleepers, for there was no time to lose. But turning to where Uncle Billy had been lying, he found him gone. A suspicion leaped to his brain, and a curse to his lips. He ran to the spot where the mules had been tethered—they were no longer there. The tracks were already rapidly disappearing in the snow.

The momentary excitement brought Mr. Oakhurst back to the fire with his usual calm. He did not waken the sleepers. The Innocent slumbered peacefully, with a smile on his good-humored, freckled face; the virgin Piney slept beside her frailer sisters as sweetly as though attended by celestial guardians; and Mr.

Oakhurst, drawing his blanket over his shoulders, stroked his mustaches and waited for the dawn. It came slowly in a whirling mist of snowflakes that dazzled and confused the eye. What could be seen of the landscape appeared magically changed. He looked over the valley, and summed up the present and future in two words, "Snowed in!"

A careful inventory of the provisions, which, fortunately for the party, had been stored within the hut, and so escaped the felonious fingers of Uncle Billy, disclosed the fact that with care and prudence they might last ten days longer. "That is," said Mr. Oakhurst *sotto voce* to the Innocent, "if you're willing to board us. If you ain't—and perhaps you'd better not—you can wait till Uncle Billy gets back with provisions." For some occult reason, Mr. Oakhurst could not bring himself to disclose Uncle Billy's rascality, and so offered the hypothesis that he had wandered from the camp and had accidentally stampeded the animals. He dropped a warning to the Duchess and Mother Shipton, who of course knew the facts of their associate's defection. "They'll find out the truth about us *all* when they find out anything," he added significantly, "and there's no good frightening them now."

Tom Simson not only put all his worldly store at the disposal of Mr. Oakhurst, but seemed to enjoy the prospect of their enforced seclusion. "We'll have a good camp for a week, and then the snow'll melt, and we'll all go back together." The cheerful gayety of the young man and Mr. Oakhurst's calm infected the others. The Innocent, with the aid of pine boughs, extemporized a thatch for the roofless cabin, and the Duchess directed Piney in the rearrangement of the interior with a taste and tact that opened the blue eyes of that provincial maiden to their fullest extent. "I reckon now you're used to fine things at Poker Flat," said Piney. The Duchess turned away sharply to conceal something that reddened her cheeks through their professional tint, and Mother Shipton requested Piney not to chatter. But when Mr. Oakhurst returned from a weary search for the trail, he heard the sound of happy laughter echoed from the rocks. He stopped in some alarm, and his thoughts first naturally reverted to the whiskey, which he had prudently cached. "And yet it don't somehow sound like whiskey," said the gambler. It was not until he caught sight of the blazing fire through the still blinding storm, and the group around it, that he settled to the conviction that it was "square fun."

Whether Mr. Oakhurst had cached his cards with the whiskey as something debarred the free access of the community, I cannot say. It was certain that, in

Mother Shipton's words, he "didn't say 'cards' once" during that evening. Haply the time was beguiled by an accordion, produced somewhat ostentatiously by Tom Simson from his pack. Notwithstanding some difficulties attending the manipulation of this instrument, Piney Woods managed to pluck several reluctant melodies from its keys, to an accompaniment by the Innocent on a pair of bone castanets. But the crowning festivity of the evening was reached in a rude camp-meeting hymn, which the lovers, joining hands, sang with great earnestness and vociferation. I fear that a certain defiant tone and Covenanter's swing to its chorus, rather than any devotional quality, caused it speedily to infect the others, who at last joined in the refrain:

I'm proud to live in the service of the Lord,
And I'm bound to die in His army.

The pines rocked, the storm eddied and whirled above the miserable group, and the flames of their altar leaped heavenward, as if in token of the vow.

At midnight the storm abated, the rolling clouds parted, and the stars glittered keenly above the sleeping camp. Mr. Oakhurst, whose professional habits had enabled him to live on the smallest possible amount of sleep, in dividing the watch with Tom Simson somehow managed to take upon himself the greater part of that duty. He excused himself to the Innocent by saying that he had "often been a week without sleep." "Doing what?" asked Tom. "Poker!" replied Oakhurst sententiously. "When a man gets a streak of luck, he don't get tired. The luck gives in first. Luck," continued the gambler reflectively, "is a mighty queer thing. All you know about it for certain is that it's bound to change. And it's finding out when it's going to change that makes you. We've had a streak of bad luck since we left Poker Flat—you come along, and slap you get into it, too. If you can hold your cards right along you're all right. For," added the gambler, with cheerful irrelevance,

I'm proud to live in the service of the Lord,
And I'm bound to die in His army.

The third day came, and the sun, looking through the white-curtained valley, saw the outcasts divide their slowly decreasing store of provisions for the morning meal. It was one of the peculiarities of that mountain climate that its rays diffused a kindly warmth over the wintry landscape, as if in regretful commiseration of the past. But it revealed drift on drift of snow piled high around the hut—a hopeless, uncharted, trackless sea of white lying below the rocky shores to which the castaways still clung. Through the marvelously clear air the smoke of the pastoral village of Poker Flat rose miles away. Mother Shipton saw it, and from a remote pinnacle of her rocky fastness hurled in that direction a final malediction. It was her last vituperative attempt, and perhaps for that reason was invested with a certain degree of sublimity. It did her good, she privately informed the Duchess. "Just you go out there and cuss, and see." She then set herself to the task of amusing "the child," as she and the Duchess were pleased to call Piney. Piney was no chicken, but it was a soothing and original theory of the pair thus to account for the fact that she didn't swear and wasn't improper.

When night crept up again through the gorges, the reedy notes of the accordion rose and fell in fitful spasms and long-drawn gasps by the flickering campfire. But music failed to fill entirely the aching void left by insufficient food, and a new diversion was proposed by Piney—storytelling. Neither Mr. Oakhurst nor his female companions caring to relate their personal experiences, this plan would have failed too, but for the Innocent. Some months before he had chanced upon a stray copy of Mr. Pope's ingenious translation of the Iliad. He now proposed to narrate the principal incidents of that poem—having thoroughly mastered the argument and fairly forgotten the words—in the current vernacular of Sandy Bar. And so for the rest of that night the Homeric demigods again walked the earth. Trojan bully and wily Greek wrestled in the winds, and the great pines in the canyon seemed to bow to the wrath of the son of Peleus. Mr. Oakhurst listened with quiet satisfaction. Most especially was he interested in the fate of Ash-heels, as the Innocent persisted in denominating the swift-footed Achilles.

So, with small food and much of Homer and the accordion, a week passed over the heads of the outcasts. The sun again forsook them, and again from leaden skies the snowflakes were sifted over the land. Day by day closer around them drew the snowy circle, until at last they looked from their prison over drifted walls of dazzling white, that towered twenty feet above their heads. It became more and more difficult to replenish their fires, even from the fallen trees beside them, now half hidden in the drifts. And yet no one complained. The lovers turned from the dreary prospect and looked into each other's eyes, and were happy. Mr. Oakhurst settled himself coolly to the losing game before him. The Duchess, more cheerful than she had been, assumed the care of Piney. Only Mother Shipton—once the strongest of the party— seemed to sicken and fade. At midnight on the tenth day she called Oakhurst to her side. "I'm going," she said, in a voice of querulous weakness, "but don't say anything about it. Don't waken the kids. Take the bundle from under my head, and open it." Mr. Oakhurst did so. It contained Mother Shipton's rations for the last week, untouched. "Give 'em to the child," she said, pointing to the sleeping Piney. "You've starved yourself," said the gambler. "That's what they call it," said the woman querulously, as she lay down again, and, turning her face to the wall, passed quietly away.

The accordion and the bones were put aside that day, and Homer was forgotten. When the body of Mother Shipton had been committed to the snow, Mr. Oakhurst took the Innocent aside, and showed him a pair of snowshoes, which he had fashioned from the old pack-saddle. "There's one chance in a hundred to save her yet," he said, pointing to Piney; "but it's there," he added, pointing toward Poker Flat. "If you can reach there in two days she's safe." "And you?" asked Tom Simson. "I'll stay here," was the curt reply.

The lovers parted with a long embrace. "You are not going, too?" said the Duchess, as she saw Mr. Oakhurst apparently waiting to accompany him. "As far as the canyon," he replied. He turned suddenly and kissed the Duchess, leaving her pallid face aflame, and her trembling limbs rigid with amazement.

Night came, but not Mr. Oakhurst. It brought the storm again and the whirling snow. Then the Duchess, feeding the fire, found that someone had quietly piled beside the hut enough fuel to last a few days longer. The tears rose to her eyes, but she hid them from Piney.

The women slept but little. In the morning, looking into each other's faces, they read their fate. Neither spoke, but Piney, accepting the position of the stronger, drew near and placed her arm around the Duchess's waist. They kept this attitude for the rest of the day. That night the storm reached its greatest fury, and, rending asunder the protecting vines, invaded the very hut.

Toward morning they found themselves unable to feed the fire, which gradually died away. As the embers slowly blackened, the Duchess crept closer to Piney, and broke the silence of many hours: "Piney, can you pray?" "No, dear," said Piney simply. The Duchess, without knowing exactly why, felt relieved, and, putting her head upon Piney's shoulder, spoke no more. And so reclining, the younger and purer pillowing the head of her soiled sister upon her virgin breast, they fell asleep.

The wind lulled as if it feared to waken them. Feathery drifts of snow, shaken from the long pine boughs, flew like white winged birds, and settled about them as they slept. The moon through the rifted clouds looked down upon what had been the camp. But all human stain, all trace of earthly travail, was hidden beneath the spotless mantle mercifully flung from above.

They slept all that day and the next, nor did they waken when voices and footsteps broke the silence of the camp. And when pitying fingers brushed the snow from their wan faces, you could scarcely have told from the equal peace that dwelt upon them which was she that had sinned. Even the law of Poker Flat recognized this, and turned away, leaving them still locked in each other's arms.

But at the head of the gulch, on one of the largest pine trees, they found the deuce of clubs pinned to the bark with a Bowie knife. It bore the following, written in pencil in a firm hand:

✝

BENEATH THIS TREE

LIES THE BODY

OF

JOHN OAKHURST

WHO STRUCK A STREAK OF BAD LUCK

BRET HARTE

ON THE 23RD OF NOVEMBER, 1850
AND
HANDED IN HIS CHECKS
ON THE 7TH OF DECEMBER, 1850

And pulseless and cold, with a Derringer by his side and a bullet in his heart, though still calm as in life, beneath the snow lay he who was at once the strongest and yet the weakest of the outcasts of Poker Flat.

MIGGLES

We were eight including the driver. We had not spoken during the passage of the last six miles, since the jolting of the heavy vehicle over the roughening road had spoiled the Judge's last poetical quotation. The tall man beside the Judge was asleep, his arm passed through the swaying strap and his head resting upon it—altogether a limp, helpless looking object, as if he had hanged himself and been cut down too late. The French lady on the back seat was asleep too, yet in a half-conscious propriety of attitude, shown even in the disposition of the handkerchief which she held to her forehead and which partially veiled her face. The lady from Virginia City, traveling with her husband, had long since lost all individuality in a wild confusion of ribbons, veils, furs, and shawls. There was no sound but the rattling of wheels and the dash of rain upon the roof. Suddenly the stage stopped and we became dimly aware of voices. The driver was evidently in the midst of an exciting colloquy with someone in the road—a colloquy of which such

41

fragments as "bridge gone," "twenty feet of water," "can't pass," were occasionally distinguishable above the storm. Then came a lull, and a mysterious voice from the road shouted the parting adjuration:

"Try Miggles'."

We caught a glimpse of our leaders as the vehicle slowly turned, of a horseman vanishing through the rain, and we were evidently on our way to Miggles'.

Who and where was Miggles? The Judge, our authority, did not remember the name, and he knew the country thoroughly. The Washoe traveler thought Miggles must keep a hotel. We only knew that we were stopped by high water in front and rear, and that Miggles was our rock of refuge. A ten-minute splashing through a tangled by-road scarcely wide enough for the stage, and we drew up before a barred and boarded gate in a wide stone wall or fence about eight feet high. Evidently Miggles', and evidently Miggles did not keep a hotel.

The driver got down and tried the gate. It was securely locked.

"Miggles! O Miggles!"

No answer.

"Migg-ells! You Miggles!" continued the driver, with rising wrath.

"Migglesy!" joined in the expressman persuasively. "O Miggy! Mig!"

But no reply came from the apparently insensate Miggles. The Judge, who had finally got the window down, put his head out and propounded a series of questions, which if answered categorically would have undoubtedly elucidated the whole mystery, but which the driver evaded by replying that "if we didn't want to sit in the coach all night we had better rise up and sing out for Miggles."

So we rose up and called on Miggles in chorus, then separately. And when we had finished, a Hibernian fellow passenger from the roof called for "Maygells!" whereat we all laughed. While we were laughing the driver cried, "Shoo!"

We listened. To our infinite amazement the chorus of "Miggles" was repeated from the other side of the wall, even to the final and supplemental "Maygells."

"Extraordinary echo!" said the Judge.

"Extraordinary d—d skunk!" roared the driver contemptuously. "Come out of that, Miggles, and show yourself! Be a man, Miggles! Don't hide in the dark; I wouldn't if I were you, Miggles," continued Yuba Bill, now dancing about in an excess of fury.

"Miggles!" continued the voice, "O Miggles!"

"My good man! Mr. Myghail!" said the Judge, softening the asperities of the name as much as possible. "Consider the inhospitality of refusing shelter from the inclemency of the weather to helpless females. Really, my dear sir," but a succession of "Miggles" ending in a burst of laughter, drowned his voice.

Yuba Bill hesitated no longer. Taking a heavy stone from the road, he battered down the gate, and with the expressman entered the enclosure. We followed. Nobody was to be seen. In the gathering darkness all that we could distinguish was that we were in a garden—from the rose bushes that scattered over us a minute spray from their dripping leaves—and before a long, rambling wooden building.

"Do you know this Miggles?" asked the Judge of Yuba Bill.

"No, nor don't want to," said Bill shortly, who felt the Pioneer Stage Company insulted in his person by the contumacious Miggles.

"But, my dear sir," expostulated the Judge, as he thought of the barred gate.

"Lookee here," said Yuba Bill, with fine irony, "hadn't you better go back and sit in the coach till yer introduced? I'm going in," and he pushed open the door of the building.

A long room, lighted only by the embers of a fire that was dying on the large hearth at its farther extremity; the walls curiously papered, and the flickering firelight bringing out its grotesque pattern; someone sitting in a large armchair by the fireplace. All this we saw as we crowded together into the room after the driver and expressman.

"Hello! Be you Miggles?" said Yuba Bill to the solitary occupant.

The figure neither spoke nor stirred. Yuba Bill walked wrathfully toward it and turned the eye of his coach-lantern upon its face. It was a man's face, prematurely old and wrinkled, with very large eyes, in which there was that expression of perfectly gratuitous solemnity which I had sometimes seen in an owl's. The large eyes wandered from Bill's face to the lantern, and finally fixed their gaze on that luminous object without further recognition.

Bill restrained himself with an effort.

"Miggles! be you deaf? You ain't dumb anyhow, you know," and Yuba Bill shook the insensate figure by the shoulder.

To our great dismay, as Bill removed his hand, the venerable stranger apparently collapsed, sinking into half his size and an undistinguishable heap of clothing.

"Well, dern my skin," said Bill, looking appealingly at us, and hopelessly retiring from the contest.

The Judge now stepped forward, and we lifted the mysterious invertebrate back into his original position. Bill was dismissed with the lantern to reconnoiter outside, for it was evident that, from the helplessness of this solitary man there must be attendants near at hand, and we all drew around the fire. The Judge, who had regained his authority, and had never lost his conversational amiability—standing before us with his back to the hearth—charged us, as an imaginary jury, as follows:

"It is evident that either our distinguished friend here has reached that condition described by Shakespeare as 'the sere and yellow leaf,' or has suffered some premature abatement of his mental and physical faculties. Whether he is really the Miggles—"

Here he was interrupted by "Miggles! O Miggles! Migglesy! Mig!" And, in fact, the whole chorus of Miggles in very much the same key as it had once before been delivered unto us.

We gazed at each other for a moment in some alarm. The Judge, in particular, vacated his position quickly, as the voice seemed to come directly over his shoulder. The cause, however, was soon discovered in a large magpie who was perched upon a shelf over the

fireplace, and who immediately relapsed into a sepul-
chral silence, which contrasted singularly with his
previous volubility. It was, undoubtedly, his voice
which we had heard in the road, and our friend in the
chair was not responsible for the discourtesy. Yuba
Bill, who reentered the room after an unsuccessful
search, was both to accept the explanation, and still
eyed the helpless sitter with suspicion. He had found a
shed in which he had put up his horses, but he came
back dripping and skeptical. "Thar ain't nobody but
him within ten mile of the shanty, and that 'ar d—d old
skeesicks knows it."

But the faith of the majority proved to be securely
based. Bill had scarcely ceased growling before we
heard a quick step upon the porch, the trailing of a wet
skirt, the door was flung open, and with a flash of
white teeth, a sparkle of dark eyes, and an utter absence of ceremony or diffidence, a young woman
entered, shut the door, and, panting, leaned back
against it.

"Oh, if you please, I'm Miggles!"

And this was Miggles! this bright-eyed, full-
throated young woman, whose wet gown of coarse
blue stuff could not hide the beauty of the feminine
curves to which it clung; from the chestnut crown of
whose head, topped by a man's oilskin sou'wester, to

47

the little feet and ankles, hidden somewhere in the recesses of her boy's brogans, all was grace—this was Miggles, laughing at us, too, in the most airy, frank, off-hand manner imaginable.

"You see, boys," said she, quite out of breath, and holding one little hand against her side, quite unheeding the speechless discomfiture of our party or the complete demoralization of Yuba Bill, whose features had relaxed into an expression of gratuitous and imbecile cheerfulness—"you see, boys, I was mor'n two miles away when you passed down the road. I thought you might pull up here, and so I ran the whole way, knowing nobody was home but Jim—and—and—I'm out of breath—and—that lets me out." And here Miggles caught her dripping oilskin hat from her head, with a mischievous swirl that scattered a shower of raindrops over us; attempted to put back her hair; dropped two hairpins in the attempt; laughed, and sat down beside Yuba Bill, with her hands crossed lightly on her lap.

The Judge recovered himself first and essayed an extravagant compliment.

"I'll trouble you for that ha'rpin," said Miggles gravely. Half a dozen hands were eagerly stretched forward; the missing hairpin was restored to its fair owner; and Miggles, crossing the room, looked keenly in the face of the invalid. The solemn eyes looked back at hers with an expression we had never seen before. Life and intelligence seemed to struggle back into the rugged face. Miggles laughed again—it was a singularly eloquent laugh—and turned her black eyes and white teeth once more towards us.

"This afflicted person is—" hesitated the Judge.

"Jim!" said Miggles.

"Your father?"

"No!"

"Brother?"

"No?"

"Husband?"

Miggles darted a quick, half-defiant glance at the two lady passengers, who I had noticed did not participate in the general masculine admiration of Miggles, and said gravely, "No, it's Jim!"

There was an awkward pause. The lady passengers moved closer to each other; the Washoe husband looked abstractedly at the fire, and the tall man apparently turned his eyes inward for self-support at this emergency. But Miggles' laugh, which was very infectious, broke the silence.

"Come," she said briskly, "you must be hungry. Who'll bear a hand to help me get tea?"

She had no lack of volunteers. In a few moments Yuba Bill was engaged like Caliban in bearing logs for this Miranda; the expressman was grinding coffee on the veranda; to myself the arduous duty of slicing bacon was assigned; and the Judge lent each man his good-humored and voluble counsel. And when Miggles, assisted by the Judge and our Hibernian "deck passenger," set the table with all the available crockery, we had become quite joyous, in spite of the rain that beat against the windows, the wind that whirled down the chimney, the two ladies who whispered together in the corner, or the magpie, who uttered a satirical and croaking commentary on their conversation from his perch above. In the now bright, blazing fire we could see that the walls were papered with illustrated journals, arranged with feminine taste and discrimination. The furniture was extemporized and adapted from candle boxes and packing cases, and covered with gay calico or the skin of some animal. The armchair of the helpless Jim was an ingenious variation of a flour barrel. There was neatness, and even a taste for the picturesque, to be seen in the few details of the long, low room.

The meal was a culinary success. But more, it was a social triumph—chiefly, I think, owing to the rare tact of Miggles in guiding the conversation, asking all the questions herself, yet bearing throughout a frankness that rejected the idea of any concealment on her own part, so that we talked of ourselves, of our prospects, of the journey, of the weather, of each other—of everything but our host and hostess. It must be confessed that Miggles' conversation was never elegant, rarely grammatical, and that at times she employed expletives the use of which had generally been yielded to our sex. But they were delivered with such a lighting up of teeth and eyes, and were usually followed by a laugh—a laugh peculiar to Miggles—so frank and honest that it seemed to clear the moral atmosphere.

Once during the meal we heard a noise like the rubbing of a heavy body against the outer walls of the house. This was shortly followed by a scratching and sniffling at the door. "That's Joaquin," said Miggles, in reply to our questioning glances; "would you like to see him?" Before we could answer she had opened the door, and disclosed a half- grown grizzly, who instantly raised himself on his haunches, with his fore paws hanging down in the popular attitude of mendicancy, and looked admiringly at Miggles, with a very singular resemblance in his manner to Yuba Bill. "That's my watch-dog," said Miggles, in explanation. "Oh, he don't bite," she added, as the two lady passengers fluttered into a corner. "Does he, old Toppy?" (the latter remark being addressed directly to the sagacious Joaquin). "I tell you what, boys," continued Miggles, after she had fed and closed the door on Ursa Minor, "you were in big luck that Joaquin wasn't hanging round when you dropped in tonight."

"Where was he?" asked the Judge.

"With me," said Miggles. "Lord love you! He trots round with me nights like as if he was a man."

We were silent for a few moments, and listened to the wind. Perhaps we all had the same picture before us—of Miggles walking through the rainy woods with her savage guardian at her side. The Judge, I remember, said something about Una and her lion; but Miggles received it, as she did other compliments, with quiet gravity. Whether she was altogether unconscious of the admiration she excited—she could hardly have been oblivious of Yuba Bill's adoration—I know not; but her very frankness suggested a perfect sexual equality that was cruelly humiliating to the younger members of our party.

The incident of the bear did not add anything in Miggles' favor to the opinions of those of her own sex who were present. In fact, the repast over, a chillness radiated from the two lady passengers that no pine boughs brought in by Yuba Bill and cast as a sacrifice upon the hearth could wholly overcome. Miggles felt it; and suddenly declaring that it was time to "turn in," offered to show the ladies to their bed in an adjoining room. "You, boys, will have to camp out here by the fire as well as you can," she added, "for thar ain't but the one room."

Our sex—by which, my dear sir, I allude of course to the stronger portion of humanity—has been generally relieved from the imputation of curiosity or a fondness for gossip. Yet I am constrained to say, that hardly had the door closed on Miggles than we crowded together, whispering, snickering, smiling, and exchanging suspicions, surmises, and a thousand speculations in regard to our pretty hostess and her singular companion. I fear that we even hustled that imbecile paralytic, who sat like a voiceless Memnon in our midst, gazing with the serene indifference of the past in his passionless eyes upon our wordy counsels. In the midst of an exciting discussion the door opened again and Miggles re-entered.

But not, apparently, the same Miggles who a few hours before had flashed upon us. Her eyes were downcast, and as she hesitated for a moment on the threshold, with a blanket on her arm, she seemed to have left behind her the frank fearlessness which had charmed us a moment before. Coming into the room, she drew a low stool beside the paralytic's chair, sat down, drew the blanket over her shoulders, and saying, "If it's all the same to you, boys, as we're rather crowded, I'll stop here tonight," took the invalid's withered hand in her own, and turned her eyes upon the dying fire. An instinctive feeling that this was only premonitory to more confidential relations, and perhaps some shame at our previous curiosity, kept us silent. The rain still heat upon the roof, wandering gusts of wind stirred the embers into momentary brightness, until, in a lull of the elements, Miggles suddenly lifted up her head, and, throwing her hair over her shoulder, turned her face upon the group and asked:

"Is there any of you that knows me?"

There was no reply.

"Think again! I lived at Marysville in '53. Everybody knew me there, and everybody had the right to know me. I kept the Polka Saloon until I came to live with Jim. That's six years ago. Perhaps I've changed some."

The absence of recognition may have disconcerted her. She turned her head to the fire again, and it was some seconds before she again spoke, and then more rapidly:

"Well, you see I thought some of you must have known me. There's no great harm done anyway. What I was going to say was this: Jim here"—she took his hand in both of hers as she spoke—"used to know me, if you didn't, and spent a heap of money upon me. I reckon he spent all he had. And one day—it's six years ago this winter—Jim came into my back room, sat down on my sofy, like as you see him in that chair, and never moved again without help. He was struck all of a heap, and never seemed to know what ailed him. The doctors came and said as how it was caused all along of his way of life—for Jim was mighty free and wild-like—and that he would never get better, and couldn't last long anyway. They advised me to send him to Frisco to the hospital, for he was no good to anyone and would be a baby all his life. Perhaps it was something in Jim's eye, perhaps it was that I never had a baby, but I said no. I was rich then, for I was popular with everybody—gentlemen like yourself, sir, came to see me—and I sold out my business and bought this yer place, because it was sort of out of the way of travel, you see, and I brought my baby here."

With a woman's intuitive tact and poetry, she had, as she spoke, slowly shifted her position so as to bring the mute figure of the ruined man between her and her audience, hiding in the shadow behind it, as if she offered it as a tacit apology for her actions. Silent and expressionless, it yet spoke for her; helpless, crushed, and smitten with the Divine thunderbolt, it still stretched an invisible arm around her.

Hidden in the darkness, but still holding his hand, she went on:

"It was a long time before I could get the hang of things about yer, for I was used to company and excitement. I couldn't get any woman to help me, and a man I dursn't trust; but what with the Indians hereabout, who'd do odd jobs for me, and having everything sent from the North Fork, Jim and I managed to worry through. The Doctor would run up from Sacramento once in a while. He'd ask to see 'Miggles' baby' as he called Jim, and when he'd go away, he'd say, 'Miggles, you're a trump—God bless you,' and it didn't seem so lonely after that. But the last time he was here he said, as he opened the door to go, 'Do you know, Miggles, your baby will grow up to be a man yet and an honor to his mother; but not here, Miggles, not here!' And I thought he went away sad—and—and"— and here Miggles' voice and head were somehow both lost completely in the shadow.

"The folks about here are very kind," said Miggles, after a pause, coming a little into the light again. "The men from the Fork used to hang around here, until they found they wasn't wanted, and the women are kind, and don't call. I was pretty lonely until I picked up Joaquin in the woods yonder one day, when he wasn't so high, and taught him to beg for his dinner; and then thar's Polly—that's the magpie—she knows no end of tricks, and makes it quite sociable of evenings with her talk, and so I don't feel like as I was the only living being about the ranch. And Jim here," said Miggles, with her old laugh again, and coming out quite into the firelight, "Jim—Why, boys, you would admire to see how much he knows for a man like him. Sometimes I bring him flowers, and he looks at 'em just as natural as if he knew 'em; and times, when we're sitting alone, I read him those things on the wall. Why, Lord!" said Miggles, with her frank laugh, "I've read him that whole side of the house this winter. There never was such a man for reading as Jim."

"Why," asked the Judge, "do you not marry this man to whom you have devoted your youthful life?"

"Well, you see," said Miggles, "it would be playing it rather low down on Jim to take advantage of his being so helpless. And then, too, if we were man and wife, now, we'd both know that I was *bound* to do what I do now of my own accord."

"But you are young yet and attractive"—

"It's getting late," said Miggles gravely, "and you'd better all turn in. Good night, boys;" and throwing the blanket over her head, Miggles laid herself down beside

57

Jim's chair, her head pillowed on the low stool that held his feet, and spoke no more. The fire slowly faded from the hearth; we each sought our blankets in silence; and presently there was no sound in the long room but the pattering of the rain upon the roof and the heavy breathing of the sleepers.

It was nearly morning when I awoke from a troubled dream. The storm had passed, the stars were shining, and through the shutterless window the full moon, lifting itself over the solemn pines without, looked into the room. It touched the lonely figure in the chair with an infinite compassion, and seemed to baptize with a shining flood the lowly head of the woman whose hair, as in the sweet old story, bathed the feet of him she loved. It even lent a kindly poetry to the rugged outline of Yuba Bill, half reclining on his elbow between them and his passengers, with savagely patient eyes keeping watch and ward. And then I fell asleep and only woke at broad day, with Yuba Bill standing over me, and "All aboard" ringing in my ears.

Coffee was waiting for us on the table, but Miggles was gone. We wandered about the house and lingered long after the horses were harnessed, but she did not return. It was evident that she wished to avoid a formal leave-taking, and had so left us to depart as we had come. After we had helped the ladies into the coach, we returned to the house and solemnly shook hands with the paralytic Jim, as solemnly setting him back into position after each handshake. Then we looked for the last time around the long low room, at the stool where Miggles had sat, and slowly took our seats in the waiting coach. The whip cracked, and we were off!

But as we reached the highroad, Bill's dexterous hand laid the six horses back on their haunches, and the stage stopped with a jerk. For there, on a little eminence beside the road, stood Miggles, her hair flying, her eyes sparkling, her white handkerchief waving, and her white teeth flashing a last "goodbye." We waved our hats in return. And then Yuba Bill, as if fearful of further fascination, madly lashed his horses forward, and we sank back in our seats.

We exchanged not a word until we reached the North Fork and the stage drew up at the Independence House. Then, the Judge leading, we walked into the barroom and took our places gravely at the bar.

"Are your glasses charged, gentlemen?" said the Judge, solemnly taking off his white hat.

They were.

"Well, then, here's to *Miggles*—God bless her!"

Perhaps He had. Who knows?

TENNESSEE'S PARTNER

I do not think that we ever knew his real name. Our ignorance of it certainly never gave us any social inconvenience, for at Sandy Bar in 1854 most men were christened anew. Sometimes these appellatives were derived from some distinctiveness of dress, as in the case of Dungaree Jack; or from some peculiarity of habit, as shown in Saleratus Bill, so called from an undue proportion of that chemical in his daily bread; or from some unlucky slip, as exhibited in The Iron Pirate, a mild, inoffensive man, who earned that baleful title by his unfortunate mispronunciation of the term iron pyrites. Perhaps this may have been the beginning of a rude heraldry; but I am constrained to think that it was because a man's real name in that day rested solely upon his own unsupported statement. "Call yourself Clifford, do you?" said Boston, addressing a timid newcomer with infinite scorn. "Hell is full of such Cliffords!" He then introduced the unfortunate man, whose name happened to be really Clifford, as

"Jaybird Charley," an unhallowed inspiration of the moment that clung to him ever after.

But to return to Tennessee's Partner, whom we never knew by any other than this relative title. That he had ever existed as a separate and distinct individuality we only learned later. It seems that in 1853 he left Poker Flat to go to San Francisco, ostensibly to procure a wife. He never got any farther than Stockton. At that place he was attracted by a young person who waited upon the table at the hotel where he took his meals. One morning he said something to her which caused her to smile not unkindly, to somewhat coquettishly break a plate of toast over his upturned, serious, simple face, and to retreat to the kitchen. He followed her, and emerged a few moments later, covered with more toast and victory. That day week they were married by a justice of the peace, and returned to Poker Flat. I am aware that something more might be made of this episode, but I prefer to tell it as it was current at Sandy Bar—in the gulches and barrooms— where all sentiment was modified by a strong sense of humor.

Of their married felicity but little is known, perhaps for the reason that Tennessee, then living with his partner, one day took occasion to say something to the bride on his own account, at which, it is said, she smiled not unkindly and chastely retreated—this time as far as Marysville, where Tennessee followed her, and where they went to housekeeping without the aid of a justice of the peace. Tennessee's Partner took the loss of his wife simply and seriously, as was his fashion. But to everybody's surprise, when Tennessee one day returned from Marysville, without his partner's wife—she having smiled and retreated with somebody else—Tennessee's Partner was the first man to shake his hand and greet him with affection. The boys who had gathered in the canyon to see the shooting were naturally indignant. Their indignation might have found vent in sarcasm but for a certain look in Tennessee's Partner's eye that indicated a lack of humorous appreciation. In fact, he was a grave man, with a steady application to practical detail which was unpleasant in a difficulty.

Meanwhile a popular feeling against Tennessee had grown up on the Bar. He was known to be a gambler; he was suspected to be a thief. In these suspicions Tennessee's Partner was equally compromised; his continued intimacy with Tennessee after the affair above quoted could only be accounted for on the hypothesis of a co-partnership of crime. At last Tennessee's guilt became flagrant. One day he overtook a stranger on his way to Red Dog. The stranger afterward related that Tennessee beguiled the time with interesting anecdote and reminiscence, but illogically concluded the interview in the following words: "And now, young man, I'll trouble you for your knife, your pistols, and your money. You see your weppings might get you into trouble at Red Dog, and your money's a temptation to the evilly disposed. I think you said your address was San Francisco. I shall endeavor to call." It may be stated here that Tennessee had a fine flow of humor, which no business preoccupation could wholly subdue.

This exploit was his last. Red Dog and Sandy Bar made common cause against the highwayman. Tennessee was hunted in very much the same fashion as his prototype, the grizzly. As the toils closed around him, he made a desperate dash through the Bar, emptying his revolver at the crowd before the Arcade Saloon, and so on up Grizzly Canyon; but at its farther extremity he was stopped by a small man on a gray horse. The men looked at each other a moment in silence. Both were fearless, both self-possessed and independent, and both types of a civilization that in the seventeenth century would have been called heroic, but in the nineteenth simply reckless.

"What have you got there? I call," said Tennessee quietly.

"Two bowers and an ace," said the stranger as quietly, showing two revolvers and a bowie-knife.

"That takes me," returned Tennessee; and, with this gambler's epigram, he threw away his useless pistol and rode back with his captor.

It was a warm night. The cool breeze which usually sprang up with the going down of the sun behind the chaparral-crested mountain was that evening withheld from Sandy Bar. The little canyon was stifling with heated resinous odors, and the decaying driftwood on the Bar sent forth faint sickening exhalations. The feverishness of day and its fierce passions still filled the camp. Lights moved restlessly along the bank of the river, striking no answering reflection from its tawny current. Against the blackness of the pines the windows of the old loft above the express office stood out staringly bright; and through their curtainless panes the loungers below could see the forms of those who were even then deciding the fate of Tennessee. And above all this, etched on the dark firmament, rose the Sierra, remote and passionless, crowned with remoter passionless stars.

The trial of Tennessee was conducted as fairly as was consistent with a judge and jury who felt themselves to some extent obliged to justify, in their verdict, the previous irregularities of arrest and indictment.

The law of Sandy Bar was implacable, but not vengeful. The excitement and personal feeling of the chase were over; with Tennessee safe in their hands, they were ready to listen patiently to any defense, which they were already satisfied was insufficient. There being no doubt in their own minds, they were willing to give the prisoner the benefit of any that might exist. Secure in the hypothesis that he ought to be hanged on general principles, they indulged him with more latitude of defense than his reckless hardihood seemed to ask. The Judge appeared to be more anxious than the prisoner, who, otherwise unconcerned, evidently took a grim pleasure in the responsibility he had created. "I don't take any hand in this yer game," had been his invariable but good-humored reply to all questions. The Judge—who was also his captor—for a moment vaguely regretted that he had not shot him "on sight" that morning, but presently dismissed this human weakness as unworthy of the judicial mind. Nevertheless, when there was a tap at the door, and it was said that Tennessee's Partner was there on behalf of the prisoner, he was admitted at once without question. Perhaps the younger members of the jury, to whom the proceedings were becoming irksomely thoughtful, hailed him as a relief.

For he was not, certainly, an imposing figure. Short and stout, with a square face, sunburned into a preternatural redness, clad in a loose duck jumper and trousers streaked and splashed with red soil, his aspect under any circumstances would have been quaint, and was now even ridiculous. As he stooped to deposit at his feet a heavy carpetbag he was carrying, it became obvious, from partially developed legends and inscriptions, that the material with which his trousers had been patched had been originally intended for a less ambitious covering. Yet he advanced with great gravity, and after shaking the hand of each person in the room with labored cordiality, he wiped his serious perplexed face on a red bandana handkerchief, a shade lighter than his complexion, laid his powerful hand upon the table to steady himself, and thus addressed the Judge:

"I was passin' by," he began, by way of apology, "and I thought I'd just step in and see how things was gittin' on with Tennessee thar, my pardner. It's a hot night. I disremember any sich weather before on the Bar."

He paused a moment, but nobody volunteering any other meteorological recollection, he again had recourse to his pocket handkerchief, and for some moments mopped his face diligently.

"Have you anything to say on behalf of the prisoner?" said the Judge finally.

"Thet's it," said Tennessee's Partner, in a tone of relief. "I come yar as Tennessee's pardner, knowing him nigh on four year, off and on, wet and dry, in luck and out o' luck. His ways ain't aller my ways, but thar ain't any p'ints in that young man, thar ain't any liveliness as he's been up to, as I don't know. And you sez to me, sez you—confidential-like, and between man and man—sez you, 'Do you know anything in his behalf?' and I sez to you, sez I—confidential-like, as between man and man—'What should a man know of his pardner?'"

"Is this all you have to say?" asked the Judge impatiently, feeling, perhaps, that a dangerous sympathy of humor was beginning to humanize the court.

"Thet's so," continued Tennessee's Partner." It ain't for me to say anything agin' him. And now, what's the case? Here's Tennessee wants money, wants it bad, and doesn't like to ask it of his old pardner. Well, what does Tennessee do? He lays for a stranger, and he fetches that stranger; and you lays for *him*, and you fetches *him*; and the honors is easy. And I put it to you, bein' a fa'r-minded man, and to you, gentlemen all, as fa'r-minded men, ef this isn't so."

67

"Prisoner," said the Judge, interrupting, "have you any questions to ask this man?"

"No! no!" continued Tennessee's Partner hastily. "I play this yer hand alone. To come down to the bedrock, it's just this: Tennessee, thar, has played it pretty rough and expensive-like on a stranger, and on this yer camp. And now, what's the fair thing? Some would say more, some would say less. Here's seventeen hundred dollars in coarse gold and a watch—it's about all my pile—and call it square!" And before a hand could be raised to prevent him, he had emptied the contents of the carpetbag upon the table.

For a moment his life was in jeopardy. One or two men sprang to their feet, several hands groped for hidden weapons, and a suggestion to "throw him from the window" was only overridden by a gesture from the Judge. Tennessee laughed. And apparently oblivious of the excitement, Tennessee's Partner improved the opportunity to mop his face again with his handkerchief.

When order was restored, and the man was made to understand, by the use of forcible figures and rhetoric, that Tennessee's offense could not be condoned by money, his face took a more serious and sanguinary hue, and those who were nearest to him noticed that his rough hand trembled slightly on the table. He hesitated a moment as he slowly returned the gold to the carpetbag, as if he had not yet entirely caught the elevated sense of justice which swayed the tribunal, and was perplexed with the belief that he had not offered enough. Then he turned to the Judge, and saying, "This yer is a lone hand, played alone, and without my pardner," he bowed to the jury and was about to withdraw, when the Judge called him back:

"If you have anything to say to Tennessee, you had better say it now."

For the first time that evening the eyes of the prisoner and his strange advocate met. Tennessee smiled, showed his white teeth, and saying, "Euchred, old man!" held out his hand. Tennessee's Partner took it in his own, and saying, "I just dropped in as I was passin' to see how things was gettin' on," let the hand passively fall, and adding that "it was a warm night," again mopped his face with his handkerchief, and without another word withdrew.

The two men never again met each other alive. For the unparalleled insult of a bribe offered to Judge Lynch—who, whether bigoted, weak, or narrow, was at least incorruptible—firmly fixed in the mind of that mythical personage any wavering determination of Tennessee's fate; and at the break of day he was marched, closely guarded, to meet it at the top of Marley's Hill.

How he met it, how cool he was, how he refused to say anything, how perfect were the arrangements of the committee, were all duly reported, with the addition of a warning moral and example to all future evildoers, in the *Red Dog Clarion,* by its editor, who was present, and to whose vigorous English I cheerfully refer the reader. But the beauty of that midsummer morning, the blessed amity of earth and air and sky, the awakened life of the free woods and hills, the joyous renewal and promise of Nature, and above all, the infinite serenity that thrilled through each, was not reported, as not being a part of the social lesson. And yet, when the weak and foolish deed was done, and a life, with its possibilities and responsibilities, had passed out of the misshapen thing that dangled between earth and sky, the birds sang, the flowers bloomed, the sun shone, as cheerily as before; and possibly the *Red Dog Clarion* was right.

Tennessee's Partner was not in the group that surrounded the ominous tree. But as they turned to disperse, attention was drawn to the singular appearance of a motionless donkey-cart halted at the side of the road. As they approached, they at once recognized the venerable "Jenny" and the two-wheeled cart as the property of Tennessee's Partner, used by him in carrying dirt from his claim; and a few paces distant the owner of the equipage himself, sitting under a buckeye tree, wiping the perspiration from his glowing face. In answer to an inquiry, he said he had come for the body of the "diseased," "if it was all the same to the committee." He didn't wish to "hurry anything;" he could "wait." He was not working that day; and when the gentlemen were done with the "diseased," he would take him. "Ef thar is any present," he added, in his simple, serious way, "as would care to jine in the fun'l, they kin come." Perhaps it was from a sense of humor, which I have already intimated was a feature of Sandy Bar. Perhaps it was from something even better than that, but two thirds of the loungers accepted the invitation at once.

It was noon when the body of Tennessee was delivered into the hands of his partner. As the cart drew up to the fatal tree, we noticed that it contained a rough oblong box—apparently made from a section of sluicing—and half filled with bark and the tassels of pine. The cart was further decorated with slips of willow and made fragrant with buckeye blossoms. When the body was deposited in the box, Tennessee's Partner drew over it a piece of tarred canvas, and gravely mounting the narrow seat in front, with his feet upon

71

the shafts, urged the little donkey forward. The equipage moved slowly on, at that decorous pace which was habitual with Jenny even under less solemn circumstances. The men—half curiously, half jestingly, but all good-humoredly—strolled along beside the cart, some in advance, some a little in the rear of the homely catafalque. But whether from the narrowing of the road or some present sense of decorum, as the cart passed on, the company fell to the rear in couples, keeping step, and otherwise assuming the external show of a formal procession. Jack Folinsbee, who had at the outset played a funeral march in dumb show upon an imaginary trombone, desisted from a lack of sympathy and appreciation—not having, perhaps, your true humorist's capacity to be content with the enjoyment of his own fun.

The way led through Grizzly Canyon, by this time clothed in funereal drapery and shadows. The redwoods, burying their moccasined feet in the red soil, stood in Indian file along the track, trailing an uncouth benediction from their bending boughs upon the passing bier. A hare, surprised into helpless inactivity, sat upright and pulsating in the ferns by the roadside as the cortege went by. Squirrels hastened to gain a secure outlook from higher boughs; and the blue-jays, spreading their wings, fluttered before them like outriders, until the outskirts of Sandy Bar were reached, and the solitary cabin of Tennessee's Partner.

Viewed under more favorable circumstances, it would not have been a cheerful place. The unpicturesque site, the rude and unlovely outlines, the unsavory details, which distinguish the nest-building of the California miner, were all here with the dreariness of decay superadded. A few paces from the cabin there was a rough enclosure, which, in the brief days of Tennessee's Partner's matrimonial felicity, had been used as a garden, but was now overgrown with fern. As we approached it, we were surprised to find that what we had taken for a recent attempt at cultivation was the broken soil about an open grave.

The cart was halted before the enclosure, and rejecting the offers of assistance with the same air of simple self-reliance he had displayed throughout, Tennessee's Partner lifted the rough coffin on his back, and deposited it unaided within the shallow grave. He then nailed down the board which served as a lid, and mounting the little mound of earth beside it, took off his hat and slowly mopped his face with his handkerchief. This the crowd felt was a preliminary to speech, and they disposed themselves variously on stumps and boulders, and sat expectant.

"When a man," began Tennessee's Partner slowly, "has been running free all day, what's the natural thing for him to do? Why, to come home. And if he ain't in a condition to go home, what can his best friend do? Why, bring him home. And here's Tennessee has been running free, and we brings him home from his wandering." He paused and picked up a fragment of quartz, rubbed it thoughtfully on his sleeve, and went on: "It ain't the first time that I've packed him on my back, as you see'd me now. It ain't the first time that I brought him to this yer cabin when he couldn't help himself; it ain't the first time that I and Jinny have waited for him on yon hill, and picked him up and so fetched him home, when he couldn't speak and didn't know me. And now that it's the last time, why"—he paused and rubbed the quartz gently on his sleeve— "you see it's sort of rough on his pardner. And now, gentlemen," he added abruptly, picking up his long-handled shovel, "the fun'l's over; and my thanks, and Tennessee's thanks, to you for your trouble."

Resisting any proffers of assistance, he began to fill in the grave, turning his back upon the crowd, that after a few moments' hesitation gradually withdrew. As they crossed the little ridge that hid Sandy Bar from view, some, looking back, thought they could see Tennessee's Partner, his work done, sitting upon the grave, his shovel between his knees, and his face buried in his red bandana handkerchief. But it was argued by others that you couldn't tell his face from his handkerchief at that distance, and this point remained undecided.

In the reaction that followed the feverish excitement of that day, Tennessee's Partner was not forgotten. A secret investigation had cleared him of any complicity in Tennessee's guilt, and left only a suspicion of his general sanity. Sandy Bar made a point of calling on him, and proffering various uncouth but well-meant kindnesses. But from that day his rude health and great strength seemed visibly to decline; and when the rainy season fairly set in, and the tiny grass- blades were beginning to peep from the rocky mound above Tennessee's grave, he took to his bed.

One night, when the pines beside the cabin were swaying in the storm and trailing their slender fingers over the roof, and the roar and rush of the swollen river were heard below, Tennessee's Partner lifted his head from the pillow, saying, "It is time to go for Tennessee; I must put Jinny in the cart;" and would have risen from his bed but for the restraint of his attendant. Struggling, he still pursued his singular fancy: "There now, steady Jinny, steady old girl. How dark it is! Look out for the ruts—and look out for him too, old gal. Sometimes, you know, when he's blind drunk, he drops down right in the trail. Keep on straight up to the pine on the top of the hill. Thar! I told you so!—thar he is—coming this way, too—all by himself, sober, and his face a-shining. Tennessee! Pardner!"

And so they met.

THE IDYL OF RED GULCH

Sandy was very drunk. He was lying under an azalea bush, in pretty much the same attitude in which he had fallen some hours before. How long he had been lying there he could not tell, and didn't care; how long he should lie there was a matter equally indefinite and unconsidered. A tranquil philosophy, born of his physical condition, suffused and saturated his moral being.

The spectacle of a drunken man, and of this drunken man in particular, was not, I grieve to say, of sufficient novelty in Red Gulch to attract attention. Earlier in the day some local satirist had erected a temporary tombstone at Sandy's head, bearing the inscription, "Effects of McCorkle's whiskey—kills at forty rods," with a hand pointing to McCorkle's saloon. But this, I imagine, was, like most local satire, personal; and was a reflection upon the unfairness of the process rather than a commentary upon the impropriety of the result. With this facetious exception, Sandy had been undisturbed. A wandering mule, released from his pack, had cropped the scant herbage beside him, and sniffed curiously at the prostrate man; a vagabond dog, with that deep sympathy which the species have for drunken men, had licked his dusty boots and curled himself up at his feet, and lay there, blinking one eye in the sunlight, with a simulation of dissipation that was ingenious and dog-like in its implied flattery of the unconscious man beside him.

Meanwhile the shadows of the pine trees had slowly swung around until they crossed the road, and their trunks barred the open meadow with gigantic parallels of black and yellow. Little puffs of red dust, lifted by the plunging hoofs of passing teams, dispersed in a grimy shower upon the recumbent man. The sun sank lower and lower, and still Sandy stirred not. And then the repose of this philosopher was disturbed, as other philosophers have been, by the intrusion of an unphilosophical sex.

"Miss Mary," as she was known to the little flock that she had just dismissed from the log schoolhouse beyond the pines, was taking her afternoon walk. Observing an unusually fine cluster of blossoms on the azalea bush opposite, she crossed the road to pluck it, picking her way through the red dust, not without certain fierce little shivers of disgust and some feline circumlocution. And then she came suddenly upon Sandy!

Of course she uttered the little staccato cry of her sex. But when she had paid that tribute to her physical weakness she became overbold and halted for a moment—at least six feet from this prostrate monster—with her white skirts gathered in her hand, ready for flight. But neither sound nor motion came from the bush. With one little foot she then overturned the satirical headboard, and muttered "Beasts!"—an epithet which probably, at that moment, conveniently classified in her mind the entire male population of Red Gulch. For Miss Mary, being possessed of certain rigid notions of her own, had not, perhaps, properly appreciated the demonstrative gallantry for which the Californian has been so justly celebrated by his brother Californians, and had, as a newcomer, perhaps fairly earned the reputation of being stuck up.

As she stood there, she noticed, also, that the slant sunbeams were heating Sandy's head to what she judged to be an unhealthy temperature, and that his hat was lying uselessly at his side. To pick it up and to place it over his face was a work requiring some courage, particularly as his eyes were open. Yet she did it and made good her retreat. But she was somewhat concerned, on looking back, to see that the hat was

79

removed, and that Sandy was sitting up and saying something.

The truth was, that in the calm depths of Sandy's mind he was satisfied that the rays of the sun were beneficial and healthful; that from childhood he had objected to lying down in a hat; that no people but condemned fools, past redemption, ever wore hats; and that his right to dispense, with them when he pleased was inalienable. This was the statement of his inner consciousness. Unfortunately, its outward expression was vague, being limited to a repetition of the following formula: "Su'shine all ri'! Wasser maar, eh? Wass up, su'shine?"

Miss Mary stopped, and, taking fresh courage from her vantage of distance, asked him if there was anything that he wanted.

"Wass up? Wasser maar?" continued Sandy, in a very high key.

"Get up, you horrid man!" said Miss Mary, now thoroughly incensed; "get up and go home."

Sandy staggered to his feet. He was six feet high, and Miss Mary trembled. He started forward a few paces and then stopped.

"Wass I go home for?" he suddenly asked, with great gravity.

"Go and take a bath," replied Miss Mary, eying his grimy person with great disfavor.

To her infinite dismay, Sandy suddenly pulled off his coat and vest, threw them on the ground, kicked off his boots, and, plunging wildly forward, darted headlong over the hill in the direction of the river.

"Goodness heavens! The man will be drowned!" said Miss Mary; and then, with feminine inconsistency, she ran back to the schoolhouse and locked herself in.

That night, while seated at supper with her hostess, the blacksmith's wife, it came to Miss Mary to ask, demurely, if her husband ever got drunk. "Abner," responded Mrs. Stidger reflectively, "Let's see! Abner hasn't been tight since last 'lection." Miss Mary would have liked to ask if he preferred lying in the sun on these occasions, and if a cold bath would have hurt him; but this would have involved an explanation, which she did not then care to give. So she contented herself with opening her gray eyes widely at the red-cheeked Mrs. Stidger—a fine specimen of Southwestern efflorescence—and then dismissed the subject altogether. The next day she wrote to her dearest friend in Boston: "I think I find the intoxicated portion of this community the least objectionable, I refer, my dear, to the men, of course. I do not know anything that could make the women tolerable."

In less than a week, Miss Mary had forgotten this episode, except that her afternoon walks took thereafter, almost unconsciously, another direction. She noticed, however, that every morning a fresh cluster of azalea blossoms appeared among the flowers on her desk. This was not strange, as her little flock were aware of her fondness for flowers, and invariably kept her desk bright with anemones, syringas, and lupines; but, on questioning them, they one and all professed ignorance of the azaleas. A few days later, Master Johnny Stidger, whose desk was nearest to the window, was suddenly taken with spasms of apparently gratuitous laughter that threatened the discipline of the school. All that Miss Mary could get from him was, that someone had been "looking in the winder." Irate and indignant, she sallied from her hive to do battle with the intruder. As she turned the corner of the schoolhouse she came plump upon the quondam drunkard, now perfectly sober, and inexpressibly sheepish and guilty-looking.

These facts Miss Mary was not slow to take a feminine advantage of, in her present humor. But it was somewhat confusing to observe, also, that the beast, despite some faint signs of past dissipation, was amiable-looking—in fact, a kind of blond Samson, whose corn-colored silken beard apparently had never yet known the touch of barber's razor or Delilah's shears. So that the cutting speech which quivered on her ready tongue died upon her lips, and she contented herself with receiving his stammering apology with supercilious eyelids and the gathered skirts of uncontamination. When she reentered the schoolroom, her eyes fell upon the azaleas with a new sense of revelation; and then she laughed, and the little people all laughed, and they were all unconsciously very happy.

It was a hot day, and not long after this, that two short-legged boys came to grief on the threshold of the school with a pail of water, which they had laboriously brought from the spring, and that Miss Mary compassionately seized the pail and started for the spring herself. At the foot of the hill a shadow crossed her path, and a blue-shirted arm dexterously but gently relieved her of her burden. Miss Mary was both embarrassed and angry. "If you carried more of that for yourself," she said spitefully to the blue arm, without deigning to raise her lashes to its owner, "you'd do better." In the submissive silence that followed she regretted the speech, and thanked him so sweetly at the door that he stumbled. Which caused the children to laugh again—a laugh in which Miss Mary joined, until the color came faintly into her pale cheek. The next day a barrel was mysteriously placed beside the door, and as mysteriously filled with fresh spring-water every morning.

Nor was this superior young person without other quiet attentions. Profane Bill, driver of the Slumgullion Stage, widely known in the newspapers for his gallantry in invariably offering the box seat to the fair sex, had excepted Miss Mary from this attention, on the ground that he had a habit of "cussin' on up grades," and gave her half the coach to herself. Jack Hamlin, a gambler, having once silently ridden with her in the same coach, afterward threw a decanter at the head of a confederate for mentioning her name in a barroom. The overdressed mother of a pupil whose paternity was doubtful had often lingered near this astute Vestal's temple, never daring to enter its sacred precincts, but content to worship the priestess from afar.

With such unconscious intervals the monotonous procession of blue skies, glittering sunshine, brief twilights, and starlit nights passed over Red Gulch. Miss Mary grew fond of walking in the sedate and proper woods. Perhaps she believed, with Mrs. Stidger, that the balsamic odors of the firs did her chest good, for certainly her slight cough was less frequent and her step was firmer; perhaps she had learned the unending lesson which the patient pines are never weary of repeating to heedful or listless ears. And so one day she planned a picnic on Buckeye Hill, and took the children with her. Away from the dusty road, the straggling shanties, the yellow ditches, the clamor of restless engines, the cheap finery of shop windows, the deeper glitter of paint and colored glass, and the thin veneering which barbarism takes upon itself in such localities, what infinite relief was theirs! The last heap of ragged rock and clay passed, the last unsightly chasm crossed—how the waiting woods opened their long files to receive them! How the children—perhaps because they had not yet grown quite away from the breast of the bounteous Mother—threw themselves face downward on her brown bosom with uncouth caresses, filling the air with their laughter; and how Miss Mary herself—felinely fastidious and entrenched as she was in the purity of spotless skirts, collar, and cuffs—forgot all, and ran like a crested quail at the head of her brood, until, romping, laughing, and panting, with a loosened braid of brown hair, a hat hanging by a knotted ribbon from her throat, she came suddenly and violently, in the heart of the forest, upon the luckless Sandy!

The explanations, apologies, and not overwise conversation that ensued need not be indicated here. It would seem, however, that Miss Mary had already established some acquaintance with this ex-drunkard. Enough that he was soon accepted as one of the party; that the children, with that quick intelligence which Providence gives the helpless, recognized a friend, and played with his blond beard and long silken mustache, and took other liberties, as the helpless are apt to do. And when he had built a fire against a tree, and had shown them other mysteries of woodcraft, their admiration knew no bounds. At the close of two such foolish, idle, happy hours he found himself lying at the feet of the schoolmistress, gazing dreamily in her face as she sat upon the sloping hillside weaving wreaths of laurel and syringa, in very much the same attitude as he had lain when first they met. Nor was the similitude greatly forced. The weakness of an easy, sensuous nature, that had found a dreamy exaltation in liquor, it is to be feared was now finding an equal intoxication in love.

I think that Sandy was dimly conscious of this himself. I know that he longed to be doing something—slaying a grizzly, scalping a savage, or sacrificing himself in some way for the sake of this sallow-faced, gray-eyed schoolmistress. As I should like to present him in a heroic attitude, I stay my hand with great difficulty at this moment, being only withheld from introducing such an episode by a strong conviction that it does not usually occur at such times. And I trust that my fairest reader, who remembers that, in a real crisis, it is always some uninteresting stranger or unromantic policeman, and not Adolphus, who rescues, will forgive the omission.

So they sat there undisturbed—the woodpeckers chattering overhead and the voices of the children coming pleasantly from the hollow below. What they said matters little. What they thought—which might have been interesting—did not transpire. The woodpeckers only learned how Miss Mary was an orphan; how she left her uncle's house to come to California for the sake of health and independence; how Sandy was an orphan too; how he came to California for excitement; how he had lived a wild life, and how he was trying to reform; and other details, which, from a woodpecker's viewpoint, undoubtedly must have seemed stupid and a waste of time. But even in such trifles was the afternoon spent; and when the children were again gathered, and Sandy, with a delicacy which the schoolmistress well understood, took leave of them quietly at the outskirts of the settlement, it had seemed the shortest day of her weary life.

As the long, dry summer withered to its roots, the school term of Red Gulch—to use a local euphuism— "dried up" also. In another day Miss Mary would be free, and for a season, at least, Red Gulch would know her no more. She was seated alone in the schoolhouse, her cheek resting on her hand, her eyes half closed in one of those daydreams in which Miss Mary, I fear, to the danger of school discipline, was lately in the habit of indulging. Her lap was full of mosses, ferns, and other woodland memories. She was so preoccupied with these and her own thoughts that a gentle tapping at the door passed unheard, or translated itself into the remembrance of far-off woodpeckers. When at last it asserted itself more distinctly, she started up with a flushed cheek and opened the door. On the threshold stood a woman, the self-assertion and audacity of whose dress were in singular contrast to her timid, irresolute bearing.

Miss Mary recognized at a glance the dubious mother of her anonymous pupil. Perhaps she was disappointed, perhaps she was only fastidious; but as she coldly invited her to enter, she half unconsciously settled her white cuffs and collar, and gathered closer her own chaste skirts. It was, perhaps, for this reason that the embarrassed stranger, after a moment's hesitation, left her gorgeous parasol open and sticking in the dust beside the door, and then sat down at the farther end of a long bench. Her voice was husky as she began:

"I heerd tell that you were goin' down to the Bay tomorrow, and I couldn't let you go until I came to thank you for your kindness to my Tommy."

Tommy, Miss Mary said, was a good boy, and deserved more than the poor attention she could give him.

"Thank you, miss; thank ye!" cried the stranger, brightening even through the color which Red Gulch knew facetiously as her "war paint," and striving, in her embarrassment, to drag the long bench nearer the schoolmistress. "I thank you, miss, for that; and if I am his mother, there ain't a sweeter, dearer, better boy lives than him. And if I ain't much as says it, thar ain't a sweeter, dearer, angeler teacher lives than he's got."

Miss Mary, sitting primly behind her desk, with a ruler over her shoulder, opened her gray eyes widely at this, but said nothing.

"It ain't for you to be complimented by the like of me, I know," she went on hurriedly. "It ain't for me to be comin' here, in broad day, to do it, either; but I come to ask a favor—not for me, miss—not for me, but for the darling boy."

Encouraged by a look in the young schoolmistress's eye, and putting her lilac-gloved hands together, the fingers downward, between her knees, she went on, in a low voice:

"You see, miss, there's no one the boy has any claim on but me, and I ain't the proper person to bring him up. I thought some, last year, of sending him away to Frisco to school, but when they talked of bringing a schoolma'am here, I waited till I saw you, and then I knew it was all right, and I could keep my boy a little longer. And, oh miss! He loves you so much; and if you could hear him talk about you in his pretty way, and if he could ask you what I ask you now, you couldn't refuse him.

"It is natural," she went on rapidly, in a voice that trembled strangely between pride and humility, "it's natural that he should take to you, miss, for his father, when I first knew him, was a gentleman—and the boy must forget me, sooner or later—and so I ain't a-goin' to cry about that. For I come to ask you to take my Tommy—God bless him for the bestest, sweetest boy that lives—to—to—take him with you."

She had risen and caught the young girl's hand in her own, and had fallen on her knees beside her.

"I've money plenty, and it's all yours and his. Put him in some good school, where you can go and see him, and help him to—to—to forget his mother. Do with him what you like. The worst you can do will be kindness to what he will learn with me. Only take him out of this wicked life, this cruel place, this home of shame and sorrow. You will! I know you will—won't you? You will—you must not, you cannot say no! You will make him as pure, as gentle as yourself; and when he has grown up, you will tell him his father's name—the name that hasn't passed my lips for years—the name of Alexander Morton, whom they call here Sandy! Miss Mary!—do not take your hand away! Miss Mary, speak to me! You will take my boy? Do not put your face from me. I know it ought not to look on such as me. Miss Mary!—my God, be merciful!—she is leaving me!"

Miss Mary had risen, and, in the gathering twilight, had felt her way to the open window. She stood there, leaning against the casement, her eyes fixed on the last rosy tints that were fading from the western sky. There was still some of its light on her pure young forehead, on her white collar, on her clasped white hands, but all fading slowly away. The suppliant had dragged herself, still on her knees, beside her.

"I know it takes time to consider. I will wait here all night; but I cannot go until you speak. Do not deny me now. You will!—I see it in your sweet face—such a face as I have seen in my dreams. I see it in your eyes, Miss Mary!—you will take my boy!"

The last red beam crept higher, suffused Miss Mary's eyes with something of its glory, flickered, and faded, and went out. The sun had set on Red Gulch. In the twilight and silence Miss Mary's voice sounded pleasantly.

"I will take the boy. Send him to me tonight."

The happy mother raised the hem of Miss Mary's skirts to her lips. She would have buried her hot face in its virgin folds, but she dared not. She rose to her feet.

"Does—this man—know of your intention?" asked Miss Mary suddenly.

"No, nor cares. He has never even seen the child to know it."

"Go to him at once—tonight—now! Tell him what you have done. Tell him I have taken his child, and tell him—he must never see—see—the child again. Wherever it may be, he must not come; wherever I may take it, he must not follow! There, go now, please—I'm weary, and—have much yet to do!"

They walked together to the door. On the threshold the woman turned.

"Good night!"

She would have fallen at Miss Mary's feet. But at the same moment the young girl reached out her arms, caught the sinful woman to her own pure breast for one brief moment, and then closed and locked the door.

It was with a sudden sense of great responsibility that Profane Bill took the reins of the Slumgullion stage the next morning, for the schoolmistress was one of his passengers. As he entered the highroad, in obedience to a pleasant voice from the inside, he suddenly reined up his horses and respectfully waited, as Tommy hopped out at the command of Miss Mary.

"Not that bush, Tommy—the next."

Tommy whipped out his new pocket-knife, and cutting a branch from a tall azalea bush, returned with it to Miss Mary. "All right now?"

"All right!"

And the stage door closed on the Idyl of Red Gulch.

BROWN OF CALAVERAS

A subdued tone of conversation and the absence of cigar smoke and boot heels at the windows of the Wingdam stagecoach made it evident that one of the inside passengers was a woman. A disposition on the part of loungers at the stations to congregate before the window and some concern in regard to the appearance of coats, hats, and collars, further indicated that she was lovely. All of which Mr. Jack Hamlin, on the box seat, noted with the smile of cynical philosophy. Not that he depreciated the sex, but that he recognized therein a deceitful element, the pursuit of which sometimes drew mankind away from the equally uncertain blandishments of poker—of which it may be remarked that Mr. Hamlin was a professional exponent.

So that, when he placed his narrow boot on the wheel and leaped down, he did not even glance at the window from which a green veil was fluttering, but lounged up and down with that listless and grave indifference of his class, which was, perhaps, the next thing

94

to good breeding. With his closely buttoned figure and self-contained air, he was a marked contrast to the other passengers, with their feverish restlessness and boisterous emotion; and even Bill Masters, a graduate of Harvard, with his slovenly dress, his overflowing vitality, his intense appreciation of lawlessness and barbarism, and his mouth filled with crackers and cheese, I fear cut but an unromantic figure beside this lonely calculator of chances, with his pale Greek face and Homeric gravity.

The driver called, "All aboard!" and Mr. Hamlin returned to the coach. His foot was upon the wheel, and his face raised to the level of the open window, when, at the same moment, what appeared to him to be the finest eyes in the world suddenly met his. He quietly dropped down again, addressed a few words to one of the inside passengers, effected an exchange of seats, and as quietly took his place inside. Mr. Hamlin never allowed his philosophy to interfere with decisive and prompt action.

I fear that this irruption of Jack cast some restraint upon the other passengers, particularly those who were making themselves most agreeable to the lady. One of them leaned forward, and apparently conveyed to her information regarding Mr. Hamlin's profession in a single epithet. Whether Mr. Hamlin heard it, or

whether he recognized in the informant a distinguished jurist, from whom, but a few evenings before,
he had won several thousand dollars, I cannot say. His
colorless face betrayed no sign; his black eyes, quietly
observant, glanced indifferently past the legal gentleman, and rested on the much more pleasing features
of his neighbor. An Indian stoicism—said to be an
inheritance from his maternal ancestor—stood him in
good service, until the rolling wheels rattled upon the
river gravel at Scott's Ferry, and the stage drew up at
the International Hotel for dinner. The legal gentleman
and a member of Congress leaped out, and stood
ready to assist the descending goddess, while Colonel
Starbottle of Siskiyou took charge of her parasol and
shawl. In this multiplicity of attention there was a momentary confusion and delay. Jack Hamlin quietly
opened the *opposite* door of the coach, took the lady's
hand, with that decision and positiveness which a hesitating and undecided sex know how to admire, and in
an instant had dexterously and gracefully swung her to
the ground and again lifted her to the platform. An audible chuckle on the box, I fear, came from that other
cynic, Yuba Bill, the driver. "Look keerfully arter that
baggage, Kernel," said the expressman, with affected
concern, as he looked after Colonel Starbottle, gloomily

bringing up the rear of the triumphant procession to the waiting room.

Mr. Hamlin did not stay for dinner. His horse was already saddled and awaiting him. He dashed over the ford, up the gravelly hill, and out into the dusty perspective of the Wingdam road, like one leaving an unpleasant fancy behind him. The inmates of dusty cabins by the roadside shaded their eyes with their hands and looked after him, recognizing the man by his horse, and speculating what "was up with Comanche Jack." Yet much of this interest centered on the horse, in a community where the time made by French Pete's mare, in his run from the Sheriff of Calaveras, eclipsed all concern in the ultimate fate of that worthy.

The sweating flanks of his gray at length recalled him to himself. He checked his speed, and turning into a byroad, sometimes used as a cutoff, trotted leisurely along, the reins hanging listlessly from his fingers. As he rode on, the character of the landscape changed and became more pastoral. Openings in groves of pine and sycamore disclosed some rude attempts at cultivation—a flowering vine trailed over the porch of one cabin, and a woman rocked her cradled babe under the roses of another. A little farther on, Mr. Hamlin came upon some bare-legged children wading in the willowy creek, and so wrought upon them with a badinage peculiar to himself, that they were embold-ened to climb up his horse's legs and over his saddle, until he was fain to develop an exaggerated ferocity of demeanor, and to escape, leaving behind some kisses and coin. And then, advancing deeper into the woods, where all signs of habitation failed, he began to sing, uplifting a tenor so singularly sweet, and shaded by a pathos so subdued and tender, that I wot the robins and linnets stopped to listen. Mr. Hamlin's voice was not cultivated; the subject of his song was some senti-mental lunacy, borrowed from the Negro minstrels; but there thrilled through all some occult quality of tone and expression that was unspeakably touching. Indeed, it was a wonderful sight to see this sentimental black-leg, with a pack of cards in his pocket and a revolver at his back, sending his voice before him through the dim woods with a plaint about his "Nelly's grave," in a way that overflowed the eyes of the listener. A sparrow hawk, fresh from his sixth victim, possibly recognizing in Mr. Hamlin a kindred spirit, stared at him in sur-prise, and was fain to confess the superiority of man. With a superior predatory capacity *he* couldn't sing.

But Mr. Hamlin presently found himself again on the highroad and at his former pace. Ditches and banks of gravel, denuded hillsides, stumps, and de-cayed trunks of trees, took the place of woodland and ravine, and indicated his approach to civilization. Then a church steeple came in sight, and he knew that he had reached home. In a few moments he was clattering down the single narrow street that lost itself in a chaotic ruin of races, ditches, and tailings at the foot of the hill, and dismounted before the gilded windows of the Magnolia saloon. Passing through the long barroom, he pushed open a green baize door, entered a dark passage, opened another door with a passkey, and found himself in a dimly lighted room, whose furniture, though elegant and costly for the locality, showed signs of abuse. The inlaid center table was overlaid with stained disks that were not contemplated in the original design, the embroidered armchairs were discolored, and the green velvet lounge, on which Mr. Hamlin threw himself, was soiled at the foot with the red soil of Wingdam.

Mr. Hamlin did not sing in his cage. He lay still, looking at a highly colored painting above him, representing a young creature of opulent charms. It occurred to him then, for the first time, that he had never seen exactly that kind of a woman, and that, if he should, he would not, probably, fall in love with her. Perhaps he was thinking of another style of beauty. But just then someone knocked at the door. Without rising, he pulled a cord that apparently shot back a bolt, for the door swung open, and a man entered.

The newcomer was broad-shouldered and robust—a vigor not borne out in the face, which, though handsome, was singularly weak and disfigured by dissipation. He appeared to be, also, under the influence of liquor, for he started on seeing Mr. Hamlin and said, "I thought Kate was here;" stammered, and seemed confused and embarrassed.

Mr. Hamlin smiled the smile which he had before worn on the Wingdam coach, and sat up, quite refreshed and ready for business.

"You didn't come up on the stage," continued the newcomer, "did you?"

"No," replied Hamlin; "I left it at Scott's Ferry. It isn't due for half an hour yet. But how's luck, Brown?"

"D—d bad," said Brown, his face suddenly assuming an expression of weak despair. "I'm cleaned out again, Jack," he continued, in a whining tone that formed a pitiable contrast to his bulky figure; "Can't you help me with a hundred till tomorrow's clean up? You see I've got to send money home to the old woman, and—you've won twenty times that amount from me."

The conclusion was, perhaps, not entirely logical, but Jack overlooked it, and handed the sum to his visitor. "The old-woman business is about played out, Brown," he added, by way of commentary; "why don't you say you want to buck ag'in' faro? You know you ain't married!"

"Fact, sir," said Brown, with a sudden gravity, as if the mere contact of the gold with the palm of the hand had imparted some dignity to his frame. "I've got a wife—a d—d good one, too, if I do say it—in the States. It's three years since I've seen her, and a year since I've writ to her. When things is about straight, and we get down to the lead, I'm going to send for her."

"And Kate?" queried Mr. Hamlin, with his previous smile.

Mr. Brown of Calaveras essayed an archness of glance to cover his confusion, which his weak face and whiskey-muddled intellect but poorly carried out, and said:

"D—n it, Jack, a man must have a little liberty, you know. But come, what do you say to a little game? Give us a show to double this hundred."

Jack Hamlin looked curiously at his fatuous friend. Perhaps he knew that the man was predestined to lose the money, and preferred that it should flow back into his own coffers rather than any other. He nodded his head, and drew his chair toward the table. At the same moment there came a rap upon the door.

"It's Kate," said Mr. Brown.

Mr. Hamlin shot back the bolt and the door opened. But, for the first time in his life, he staggered to his feet utterly unnerved and abashed, and for the first time in his life the hot blood crimsoned his color-less cheeks to his forehead. For before him stood the lady he had lifted from the Wingdam coach, whom Brown, dropping his cards with a hysterical laugh, greeted as:

"My old woman, by thunder!"

They say that Mrs. Brown burst into tears and re-proaches of her husband. I saw her in 1857 at Marysville and disbelieve the story. And the *Wingdam Chronicle* of the next week, under the head of "Touching Reunion," said: "One of those beautiful and touching incidents, peculiar to California life, occurred last week in our city. The wife of one of Wingdam's eminent pio-neers, tired of the effete civilization of the East and its inhospitable climate, resolved to join her noble hus-band upon these golden shores. Without informing him of her intention, she undertook the long journey, and arrived last week. The joy of the husband may be easier imagined than described. The meeting is said to have been indescribably affecting. We trust her example may be followed."

Whether owing to Mrs. Brown's influence, or to some more successful speculations, Mr. Brown's financial fortune from that day steadily improved. He bought out his partners in the "Nip and Tuck" lead, with money which was said to have been won at poker a week or two after his wife's arrival, but which rumor, adopting Mrs. Brown's theory that Brown had forsworn the gaming-table, declared to have been furnished by Mr. Jack Hamlin. He built and furnished the Wingdam House, which pretty Mrs. Brown's great popularity kept overflowing with guests. He was elected to the Assembly, and gave largess to churches. A street in Wingdam was named in his honor.

Yet it was noted that in proportion as he waxed wealthy and fortunate, he grew pale, thin, and anxious. As his wife's popularity increased, he became fretful and impatient. The most uxorious of husbands, he was absurdly jealous. If he did not interfere with his wife's social liberty, it was because it was maliciously whispered that his first and only attempt was met by an outburst from Mrs. Brown that terrified him into silence. Much of this kind of gossip came from those of her own sex whom she had supplanted in the chivalrous attentions of Wingdam, which, like most popular chivalry, was devoted to an admiration of power, whether of masculine force or feminine beauty. It should be remembered, too, in her extenuation, that, since her arrival, she had been the unconscious priestess of a mythological worship, perhaps not more ennobling to her womanhood than that which distinguished an older Greek democracy. I think that Brown was dimly conscious of this. But his only confidant was Jack Hamlin, whose infelix reputation naturally precluded any open intimacy with the family, and whose visits were infrequent.

It was midsummer and a moonlit night, and Mrs. Brown, very rosy, large-eyed, and pretty, sat upon the piazza, enjoying the fresh incense of the mountain breeze, and, it is to be feared, another incense which was not so fresh nor quite as innocent. Beside her sat Colonel Starbottle and Judge Boompointer, and a later addition to her court in the shape of a foreign tourist. She was in good spirits.

"What do you see down the road?" inquired the gallant Colonel, who had been conscious, for the last few minutes, that Mrs. Brown's attention was diverted.

"Dust," said Mrs. Brown, with a sigh. "Only Sister Anne's flock of sheep."

The Colonel, whose literary recollections did not extend farther back than last week's paper, took a more practical view. "It ain't sheep," he continued; "it's a horseman. Judge, ain't that Jack Hamlin's gray?"

But the Judge didn't know; and, as Mrs. Brown suggested the air was growing too cold for further investigations, they retired to the parlor.

Mr. Brown was in the stable, where he generally retired after dinner. Perhaps it was to show his contempt for his wife's companions; perhaps, like other weak natures, he found pleasure in the exercise of absolute power over inferior animals. He had a certain gratification in the training of a chestnut mare, whom he could beat or caress as pleased him, which he couldn't do with Mrs. Brown. It was here that he recognized a certain gray horse which had just come in, and, looking a little farther on, found his rider. Brown's greeting was cordial and hearty; Mr. Hamlin's somewhat restrained. But, at Brown's urgent request, he followed him up the back stairs to a narrow corridor, and thence to a small room looking out upon the stable-yard. It was plainly furnished with a bed, a table, a few chairs, and a rack for guns and whips.

"This yer's my home, Jack," said Brown with a sigh, as he threw himself upon the bed and motioned his companion to a chair. "Her room's t' other end of

the hall. It's more'n six months since we've lived together, or met, except at meals. It's mighty rough
papers on the head of the house, ain't it?" he said with
a forced laugh. "But I'm glad to see you, Jack, d—d
glad," and he reached from the bed, and again shook
the unresponsive hand of Jack Hamlin.

"I brought ye up here, for I didn't want to talk in
the stable; though, for the matter of that, it's all round
town. Don't strike a light. We can talk here in the
moonshine. Put up your feet on that winder and sit
here beside me. Thar's whiskey in that jug."

Mr. Hamlin did not avail himself of the information.
Brown of Calaveras turned his face to the wall, and
continued:

"If I didn't love the woman, Jack, I wouldn't mind.
But it's loving her, and seeing her day arter day goin'
on at this rate, and no one to put down the brake; that's
what gits me! But I'm glad to see ye, Jack, d—d glad."

In the darkness he groped about until he had
found and wrung his companion's hand again. He
would have detained it, but Jack slipped it into the buttoned breast of his coat, and asked listlessly, "How
long has this been going on?"

"Ever since she came here; ever since the day she
walked into the Magnolia. I was a fool then, Jack; I'm a

fool now; but I didn't know how much I loved her till then. And she hasn't been the same woman since.

"But that ain't all, Jack, and it's what I wanted to see you about, and I'm glad you've come. It ain't that she doesn't love me anymore; it ain't that she fools with every chap that comes along; for perhaps I staked her love and lost it, as I did everything else at the Magnolia; and perhaps foolin' is nateral to some women, and thar ain't no great harm done, 'cept to the fools. But, Jack, I think—I think she loves somebody else. Don't move, Jack! don't move; if your pistol hurts ye, take it off.

"It's been more'n six months now that she's seemed unhappy and lonesome, and kinder nervous and scared-like. And sometimes I've ketched her lookin' at me sort of timid and pitying. And she writes to somebody. And for the last week she's been gathering her own things—trinkets, and furbelows, and jew'lry—and, Jack, I think she's goin' off. I could stand all but that. To have her steal away like a thief!" He put his face downward to the pillow, and for a few moments there was no sound but the ticking of a clock on the mantel. Mr. Hamlin lit a cigar, and moved to the open window. The moon no longer shone into the room, and the bed and its occupant were in shadow. "What shall I do, Jack?" said the voice from the darkness.

The answer came promptly and clearly from the window side, "Spot the man, and kill him on sight."

"But, Jack—"

"He's took the risk!"

"But will that bring *her* back?"

Jack did not reply, but moved from the window towards the door.

"Don't go yet, Jack; light the candle and sit by the table. It's a comfort to see ye, if nothin' else."

Jack hesitated and then complied. He drew a pack of cards from his pocket and shuffled them, glancing at the bed. But Brown's face was turned to the wall. When Mr. Hamlin had shuffled the cards, he cut them, and dealt one card on the opposite side of the table towards the bed, and another on his side of the table for himself. The first was a deuce; his own card a king. He then shuffled and cut again. This time "dummy" had a queen and himself a four-spot. Jack brightened up for the third deal. It brought his adversary a deuce and himself a king again. "Two out of three," said Jack audibly.

"What's that, Jack?" said Brown.

"Nothing."

Then Jack tried his hand with dice; but he always threw sixes and his imaginary opponent aces. The force of habit is sometimes confusing.

Meanwhile some magnetic influence in Mr. Hamlin's presence, or the anodyne of liquor, or both, brought surcease of sorrow, and Brown slept. Mr. Hamlin moved his chair to the window and looked out on the town of Wingdam, now sleeping peacefully, its harsh outlines softened and subdued, its glaring colors mellowed and sobered in the moonlight that flowed over all. In the hush he could hear the gurgling of water in the ditches and the sighing of the pines beyond the hill. Then he looked up at the firmament, and as he did so a star shot across the twinkling field. Presently another, and then another. The phenomenon suggested to Mr. Hamlin a fresh augury. If in another fifteen minutes another star should fall—He sat there, watch in hand, for twice that time, but the phenomenon was not repeated.

The clock struck two, and Brown still slept. Mr. Hamlin approached the table and took from his pocket a letter, which he read by the flickering candlelight. It contained only a single line, written in pencil, in a woman's hand:

"Be at the corral with the buggy at three."

The sleeper moved uneasily and then awoke. "Are you there, Jack?"

"Yes."

"Don't go yet. I dreamed just now, Jack, dreamed of old times. I thought that Sue and me was being married agin, and that the parson, Jack, was—who do you think?—you!"

The gambler laughed, and seated himself on the bed, the paper still in his hand.

"It's a good sign, ain't it?" queried Brown.

"I reckon! Say, old man, hadn't you better get up?"

The "old man," thus affectionately appealed to, rose, with the assistance of Hamlin's outstretched hand.

"Smoke?"

Brown mechanically took the proffered cigar.

"Light?"

Jack had twisted the letter into a spiral, lit it, and held it for his companion. He continued to hold it until it was consumed, and dropped the fragment—a fiery star—from the open window. He watched it as it fell, and then returned to his friend.

"Old man," he said, placing his hands upon Brown's shoulders, "in ten minutes I'll be on the road, and gone like that spark. We won't see each other agin; but, before I go, take a fool's advice: sell out all you've got, take your wife with you, and quit the country. It ain't no place for you nor her. Tell her she must go; make her go if she won't. Don't whine because you can't be a saint and she ain't an angel. Be a man, and treat her like a woman. Don't be a d—d fool. Goodbye."

He tore himself from Brown's grasp and leaped down the stairs like a deer. At the stable door he collared the half-sleeping hostler, and backed him against the wall. "Saddle my horse in two minutes, or I'll—" The ellipsis was frightfully suggestive.

"The missis said you was to have the buggy," stammered the man.

"D—n the buggy!"

The horse was saddled as fast as the nervous hands of the astounded hostler could manipulate buckle and strap.

"Is anything up, Mr. Hamlin?" said the man, who, like all his class, admired the élan of his fiery patron, and was really concerned in his welfare.

"Stand aside!"

The man fell back. With an oath, a bound, and clatter, Jack was into the road. In another moment, to the man's half-awakened eyes, he was but a moving cloud of dust in the distance, towards which a star just loosed from its brethren was trailing a stream of fire.

But early that morning the dwellers by the Wingdam turnpike, miles away, heard a voice, pure as a skylark's, singing afield. They who were asleep turned over on their rude couches to dream of youth, and love, and olden days. Hard-faced men and anxious gold seekers, already at work, ceased their labors and leaned upon their picks to listen to a romantic vagabond ambling away against the rosy sunrise.

THE LEGEND OF MONTE DEL DIABLO

The cautious reader will detect a lack of authenticity in the following pages. I am not a cautious reader myself, yet I confess with some concern to the absence of much documentary evidence in support of the singular incident I am about to relate. Disjointed memoranda, the proceedings of *ayuntamientos* and early departmental *juntas,* with other records of a primitive and superstitious people, have been my inadequate authorities. It is but just to state, however, that though this particular story lacks corroboration, in ransacking the Spanish archives of Upper California, I have met with many more surprising and incredible stories, attested and supported to a degree that would have placed this legend beyond a cavil or doubt. I have, also, never lost faith in the legend myself, and in so doing have profited much from the examples of divers grant claimants, who have often jostled me in their more practical researches, and who have my sincere sympathy at the skepticism of a modern hard-headed and practical world.

For many years after Father Junipero Serro first
rang his bell in the wilderness of Upper California, the
spirit which animated that adventurous priest did not
wane. The conversion of the heathen went on rapidly
in the establishment of Missions throughout the land.
So sedulously did the good Fathers set about their
work, that around their isolated chapels there presently arose adobe huts, whose mud-plastered and
savage tenants partook regularly of the provisions,
and occasionally of the Sacrament, of their pious hosts.
Nay, so great was their progress, that one zealous
Padre is reported to have administered the Lord's
Supper one Sabbath morning to "over three hundred
heathen savages." It was not to be wondered that the
Enemy of Souls, being greatly incensed thereat, and
alarmed at his decreasing popularity, should have griev-
ously tempted and embarrassed these Holy Fathers, as
we shall presently see.

Yet they were happy, peaceful days for California.
The vagrant keels of prying Commerce had not as yet
ruffled the lordly gravity of her bays. No torn and
ragged gulch betrayed the suspicion of golden treasure. The wild oats drooped idly in the morning heat, or
wrestled with the afternoon breezes. Deer and ante-
lope dotted the plain. The watercourses brawled in
their familiar channels, nor dreamed of ever shifting

their regular tide. The wonders of the Yosemite and Calaveras were as yet unrecorded. The Holy Fathers noted little of the landscape beyond the barbaric prodigality with which the quick soil repaid the sowing. A new conversion, the advent of a Saint's day, or the baptism of an Indian baby, was at once the chronicle and marvel of their day.

At this blissful epoch there lived at the Mission of San Pablo Father José Antonio Haro, a worthy brother of the Society of Jesus. He was of tall and cadaverous aspect. A somewhat romantic history had given a poetic interest to his lugubrious visage. While a youth, pursuing his studies at famous Salamanca, he had become enamored of the charms of Doña Carmen de Torrencevara, as that lady passed to her matutinal devotions. Untoward circumstances, hastened, perhaps, by a wealthier suitor, brought this amour to a disastrous issue; and Father José entered a monastery, taking upon himself the vows of celibacy. It was here that his natural fervor and poetic enthusiasm conceived expression as a missionary. A longing to convert the uncivilized heathen succeeded his frivolous earthly passion, and a desire to explore and develop unknown fastnesses continually possessed him. In his flashing eye and somber exterior was

115

detected a singular commingling of the discreet Las Casas and the impetuous Balboa.

Fired by this pious zeal, Father José went forward in the van of Christian pioneers. On reaching Mexico, he obtained authority to establish the Mission of San Pablo. Like the good Junipero, accompanied only by an acolyte and muleteer, he unsaddled his mules in a dusky canyon, and rang his bell in the wilderness. The savages—a peaceful, inoffensive, and inferior race— presently flocked around him. The nearest military post was far away, which contributed much to the security of these pious pilgrims, who found their open trustfulness and amiability better fitted to repress hostility than the presence of an armed, suspicious, and brawling soldiery. So the good Father José said matins and prime, mass and vespers, in the heart of sin and heathenism, taking no heed to himself, but looking only to the welfare of the Holy Church. Conversions soon followed, and, on the 7th of July, 1760, the first Indian baby was baptized—an event which, as Father José piously records, "exceeds the richness of gold or precious jewels or the chancing upon the Ophir of Solomon." I quote this incident as best suited to show the ingenious blending of poetry and piety which distinguished Father José's record.

The Mission of San Pablo progressed and prospered until the pious founder thereof, like the infidel Alexander, might have wept that there were no more heathen worlds to conquer. But his ardent and enthusiastic spirit could not long brook an idleness that seemed begotten of sin; and one pleasant August morning, in the year of grace 1770, Father José issued from the outer court of the Mission building, equipped to explore the field for new missionary labors.

Nothing could exceed the quiet gravity and unpretentiousness of the little cavalcade. First rode a stout muleteer, leading a pack mule laden with the provisions of the party, together with a few cheap crucifixes and hawks' bells. After him came the devout Padre José, bearing his breviary and cross, with a black serape thrown around his shoulders; while on either side trotted a dusky convert, anxious to show a proper sense of their regeneration by acting as guides into the wilds of their heathen brethren. Their new condition was agreeably shown by the absence of the usual mud plaster, which in their unconverted state they assumed to keep away vermin and cold. The morning was bright and propitious. Before their departure, mass had been said in the chapel, and the protection of St. Ignatius invoked against all contingent evils, but especially against bears, which, like the fiery dragons of

117

old, seemed to cherish unconquerable hostility to the Holy Church.

As they wound through the canyon, charming birds disported upon boughs and sprays, and sober quails piped from the alders; the willowy water courses gave a musical utterance, and the long grass whispered on the hillside. On entering the deeper defiles, above them towered dark green masses of pine, and occasionally the madroño shook its bright scarlet berries. As they toiled up many a steep ascent, Father José sometimes picked up fragments of scoria, which spoke to his imagination of direful volcanoes and impending earthquakes. To the less scientific mind of the muleteer Ignacio they had even a more terrifying significance; and he once or twice snuffed the air suspiciously, and declared that it smelt of sulphur. So the first day of their journey wore away, and at night they encamped without having met a single heathen face.

It was on this night that the Enemy of Souls appeared to Ignacio in an appalling form. He had retired to a secluded part of the camp and had sunk upon his knees in prayerful meditation, when he looked up and perceived the Arch-Fiend in the likeness of a monstrous bear. The Evil One was seated on his hind legs immediately before him, with his fore paws joined together just below his black muzzle. Wisely conceiving this remarkable attitude to be in mockery and derision of his devotions, the worthy muleteer was transported with fury. Seizing an arquebuse, he instantly closed his eyes and fired. When he had recovered from the effects of the terrific discharge, the apparition had disappeared. Father José, awakened by the report, reached the spot only in time to chide the muleteer for wasting powder and ball in a contest with one whom a single *ave* would have been sufficient to utterly discomfit. What further reliance he placed on Ignacio's story is not known; but, in commemoration of a worthy Californian custom, the place was called *La Cañada de la Tentación del Pio Muletero,* or *The Glen of the Temptation of the Pious Muleteer,* a name which it retains to this day.

The next morning the party, issuing from a narrow gorge, came upon a long valley, sear and burnt with the shadeless heat. Its lower extremity was lost in a fading line of low hills, which, gathering might and volume toward the upper end of the valley, upheaved a stupendous bulwark against the breezy North. The peak of this awful spur was just touched by a fleecy cloud that shifted to and fro like a banneret. Father José gazed at it with mingled awe and admiration. By a singular coincidence, the muleteer Ignacio uttered the simple ejaculation, "Diablo!"

As they penetrated the valley, they soon began to miss the agreeable life and companionable echoes of the canyon they had quitted. Huge fissures in the parched soil seemed to gape as with thirsty mouths. A few squirrels darted from the earth, and disappeared as mysteriously before the jingling mules. A gray wolf trotted leisurely along just ahead. But whichever way Father José turned, the mountain always asserted itself and arrested his wandering eye. Out of the dry and arid valley, it seemed to spring into cooler and bracing life. Deep cavernous shadows dwelt along its base; rocky fastnesses appeared midway of its elevation; and on either side huge black hills diverged like massy roots from a central trunk. His lively fancy pictured these hills peopled with a majestic and intelligent race of savages; and looking into futurity, he already saw a monstrous cross crowning the dome-like summit. Far different were the sensations of the muleteer, who saw in those awful solitudes only fiery dragons, colossal bears and breakneck trails. The converts, Concepcion and Incarnacion, trotting modestly beside the Padre, recognized, perhaps, some manifestation of their former weird mythology.

At nightfall they reached the base of the mountain. Here Father José unpacked his mules, said vespers, and, formally ringing his bell, called upon the Gentiles within hearing to come and accept the Holy Faith. The echoes of the black frowning hills around him caught up the pious invitation, and repeated it at intervals; but no Gentiles appeared that night. Nor were the devotions of the muleteer again disturbed, although he afterward asserted, that, when the Father's exhortation was ended, a mocking peal of laughter came from the mountain. Nothing daunted by these intimations of the near hostility of the Evil One, Father José declared his intention to ascend the mountain at early dawn; and before the sun rose the next morning he was leading the way.

The ascent was in many places difficult and dangerous. Huge fragments of rock often lay across the trail, and after a few hours' climbing they were forced to leave their mules in a little gully, and continue the ascent afoot. Unaccustomed to such exertion, Father José often stopped to wipe the perspiration from his thin cheeks. As the day wore on, a strange silence oppressed them. Except the occasional pattering of a squirrel, or a rustling in the chamisal bushes, there were no signs of life. The half-human print of a bear's foot sometimes appeared before them, at which Ignacio always crossed himself piously. The eye was sometimes cheated by a dripping from the rocks, which on closer inspection proved to be a resinous oily liquid with an abominable sulphurous smell. When they were within a short distance of the summit, the discreet Ignacio, selecting a sheltered nook for the camp, slipped aside and busied himself in preparations for the evening, leaving the Holy Father to continue the ascent alone. Never was there a more thoughtless act of prudence, never a more imprudent piece of caution. Without noticing the desertion, buried in pious reflection, Father José pushed mechanically on, and, reaching the summit, cast himself down and gazed upon the prospect.

Below him lay a succession of valleys opening into each other like gentle lakes, until they were lost to the southward. Westerly the distant range hid the bosky cañada which sheltered the mission of San Pablo. In the farther distance the Pacific Ocean stretched away, bearing a cloud of fog upon its bosom, which crept through the entrance of the bay, and rolled thickly between him and the northeastward; the same fog hid the base of mountain and the view beyond. Still, from time to time the fleecy veil parted, and timidly disclosed charming glimpses of mighty rivers, mountain defiles, and rolling plains, sear with ripened oats, and bathed in the glow of the setting sun. As Father José gazed, he was penetrated with a pious longing. Already his imagination, filled with enthusiastic conceptions, beheld all that vast expanse gathered under the mild sway of the Holy Faith, and peopled with zealous converts. Each little knoll in fancy became crowned with a chapel; from each dark canyon gleamed the white walls of a mission building. Growing bolder in his enthusiasm, and looking farther into futurity, he beheld a new Spain rising on these savage shores. He already saw the spires of stately cathedrals, the domes of palaces, vineyards, gardens, and groves. Convents, half hid among the hills, peeping from plantations of branching limes; and long processions of chanting nuns wound through the defiles. So completely was the good Father's conception of the future confounded with the past, that even in their choral strain the well-remembered accents of Carmen struck his ear. He was busied in these fanciful imaginings, when suddenly over that extended prospect the faint, distant tolling of a bell rang sadly out and died. It was the Angelus. Father José listened with superstitious exaltation. The mission of San Pablo was far away, and the sound must have been some miraculous omen. But never before, to his enthusiastic sense, did the sweet seriousness of this angelic symbol come with such strange significance.

123

With the last faint peal, his glowing fancy seemed to cool; the fog closed in below him, and the good Father remembered he had not had his supper. He had risen and was wrapping his serape around him, when he perceived for the first time that he was not alone.

Nearly opposite, and where should have been the faithless Ignacio, a grave and decorous figure was seated. His appearance was that of an elderly hidalgo, dressed in mourning, with mustaches of iron-gray carefully waxed and twisted around a pair of lantern jaws. The monstrous hat and prodigious feather, the enormous ruff and exaggerated trunk hose, contrasted with a frame shriveled and wizened, all belonged to a century previous. Yet Father José was not astonished. His adventurous life and poetic imagination, continually on the lookout for the marvelous, gave him a certain advantage over the practical and material minded. He instantly detected the diabolical quality of his visitant, and was prepared. With equal coolness and courtesy he met the cavalier's obeisance.

"I ask your pardon, Sir Priest," said the stranger, "for disturbing your meditations. Pleasant they must have been, and right fanciful, I imagine, when occasioned by so fair a prospect."

"Worldly, perhaps, Sir Devil, for such I take you to be," said the Holy Father, as the stranger bowed his black plumes to the ground; "worldly, perhaps; for it hath pleased Heaven to retain even in our regenerated state much that pertaineth to the flesh, yet still, I trust, not without some speculation for the welfare of the Holy Church. In dwelling upon yon fair expanse, mine eyes have been graciously opened with prophetic inspiration, and the promise of the heathen as an inheritance hath marvelously recurred to me. For there can be none lack such diligence in the True Faith, but may see that even the conversion of these pitiful salvages hath a meaning. As the blessed St. Ignatius discreetly observes," continued Father José, clearing his throat and slightly elevating his voice, "'the heathen is given to the warriors of Christ, even as the pearls of rare discovery which gladden the hearts of shipmen.' Nay, I might say—"

But here the stranger, who had been wrinkling his brows and twisting his mustaches with well-bred patience, took advantage of an oratorical pause:

"It grieves me, Sir Priest, to interrupt the current of your eloquence as discourteously as I have already broken your meditations; but the day already waneth to night. I have a matter of serious import to make with you, could I entreat your cautious consideration a few moments."

125

Father José hesitated. The temptation was great, and the prospect of acquiring some knowledge of the Great Enemy's plans not the least trifling object. And if the truth must be told, there was a certain decorum about the stranger that interested the Padre. Though well aware of the protean shapes the Arch-Fiend could assume, and though free from the weaknesses of the flesh, Father José was not above the temptations of the spirit. Had the Devil appeared, as in the case of the pious St. Anthony, in the likeness of a comely damsel, the good Father, with his certain experience of the deceitful sex, would have whisked her away in the saying of a paternoster. But there was, added to the security of age, a grave sadness about the stranger—a thoughtful consciousness as of being at a great moral disadvantage—which at once decided him on a magnanimous course of conduct.

The stranger then proceeded to inform him, that he had been diligently observing the Holy Father's triumphs in the valley. That, far from being greatly exercised thereat, he had been only grieved to see so enthusiastic and chivalrous an antagonist wasting his zeal in a hopeless work. For, he observed, the issue of the great battle of Good and Evil had been otherwise settled, as he would presently show him. "It wants but a few moments of night," he continued, "and over this interval of twilight, as you know, I have been given complete control. Look to the West."

As the Padre turned, the stranger took his enormous hat from his head, and waved it three times before him. At each sweep of the prodigious feather, the fog grew thinner, until it melted impalpably away, and the former landscape returned, yet warm with the glowing sun. As Father José gazed, a strain of martial music arose from the valley, and issuing from a deep canyon, the good Father beheld a long cavalcade of gallant cavaliers, habited like his companion. As they swept down the plain, they were joined by like processions, that slowly defiled from every ravine and canyon of the mysterious mountain. From time to time the peal of a trumpet swelled fitfully upon the breeze; the cross of Santiago glittered, and the royal banners of Castile and Aragon waved over the moving column. So they moved on solemnly toward the sea, where, in the distance, Father José saw stately caravels, bearing the same familiar banner, awaiting them. The good Padre gazed with conflicting emotions, and the serious voice of the stranger broke the silence.

"Thou hast beheld, Sir Priest, the fading footprints of adventurous Castile. Thou hast seen the declining glory of old Spain—declining as yonder brilliant sun. The scepter she hath wrested from the heathen is fast

127

dropping from her decrepit and fleshless grasp. The children she hath fostered shall know her no longer. The soil she hath acquired shall be lost to her as irrevocably as she herself hath thrust the Moor from her own Granada."

The stranger paused, and his voice seemed broken by emotion; at the same time, Father José, whose sympathizing heart yearned toward the departing banners, cried in poignant accents:

"Farewell, ye gallant cavaliers and Christian soldiers! Farewell, thou, Nuñes de Balboa! Thou, Alonzo de Ojeda! and thou, most venerable Las Casas! Farewell, and may Heaven prosper still the seed ye left behind!"

Then turning to the stranger, Father José beheld him gravely draw his pocket handkerchief from the basket hilt of his rapier, and apply it decorously to his eyes.

"Pardon this weakness, Sir Priest," said the cavalier, apologetically; "but these worthy gentlemen were ancient friends of mine, and have done me many a delicate service—much more, perchance, than these poor sables may signify," he added, with a grim gesture toward the mourning suit he wore.

Father José was too much preoccupied in reflection to notice the equivocal nature of this tribute, and, after a few moments' silence, said, as if continuing his thought:

"But the seed they have planted shall thrive and prosper on this fruitful soil."

As if answering the interrogatory, the stranger turned to the opposite direction, and, again waving his hat, said, in the same serious tone, "Look to the East!"

The Father turned, and, as the fog broke away before the waving plume, he saw that the sun was rising. Issuing with its bright beams through the passes of the snowy mountains beyond, appeared a strange and motley crew. Instead of the dark and romantic visages of his last phantom train, the Father beheld with strange concern the blue eyes and flaxen hair of a Saxon race. In place of martial airs and musical utterance, there rose upon the ear a strange din of harsh gutturals and singular sibilation. Instead of the decorous tread and stately mien of the cavaliers of the former vision, they came pushing, bustling, panting, and swaggering. And as they passed, the good Father noticed that giant trees were prostrated as with the breath of a tornado, and the bowels of the earth were torn and rent as with a convulsion. And Father José looked in vain for holy cross or Christian symbol; there was but one that seemed an ensign, and he crossed himself with holy horror as he perceived it bore the effigy of a bear.

"Who are these swaggering Ishmaelites?" he asked, with something of asperity in his tone.

The stranger was gravely silent.

"What do they here, with neither cross nor holy symbol?" he again demanded.

"Have you the courage to see, Sir Priest?" responded the stranger, quietly.

Father José felt his crucifix, as a lonely traveler might his rapier, and assented.

"Step under the shadow of my plume," said the stranger.

Father José stepped beside him, and they instantly sank through the earth.

When he opened his eyes, which had remained closed in prayerful meditation during his rapid descent, he found himself in a vast vault, bespangled overhead with luminous points like the starred firmament. It was also lighted by a yellow glow that seemed to proceed from a mighty sea or lake that occupied the center of the chamber. Around this subterranean sea dusky figures flitted, bearing ladles filled with the yellow fluid, which they had replenished from its depths. From this lake diverging streams of the same mysterious flood penetrated like mighty rivers the cavernous distance. As they walked by the banks of this glittering Styx, Father José perceived how the liquid stream at certain places became solid. The ground was strewn with glittering flakes. One of these the Padre picked up and curiously examined. It was virgin gold.

An expression of discomfiture overcast the good Father's face at this discovery; but there was trace neither of malice nor satisfaction in the stranger's air, which was still of serious and fateful contemplation. When Father José recovered his equanimity, he said, bitterly:

"This, then, Sir Devil, is your work! This is your deceitful lure for the weak souls of sinful nations! So would you replace the Christian grace of holy Spain!"

"This is what must be," returned the stranger, gloomily. "But listen, Sir Priest. It lies with you to avert the issue for a time. Leave me here in peace. Go back to Castile, and take with you your bells, your images, and your missions. Continue here, and you only precipitate results. Stay! Promise me you will do this, and you shall not lack that which will render your old age an ornament and a blessing;" and the stranger motioned significantly to the lake.

It was here, the legend discreetly relates, that the Devil showed—as he always shows sooner or later—his cloven hoof. The worthy Padre, sorely perplexed by his threefold vision, and, if the truth must be told, a little nettled at this wresting away of the glory of holy Spanish discovery, had shown some hesitation. But the unlucky bribe of the Enemy of Souls touched his Castilian spirit. Starting back in deep disgust, he brandished his crucifix in the face of the unmasked Fiend, and in a voice that made the dusky vault resound, cried:

"Avaunt thee, Sathanas! Diabolus, I defy thee! What! Wouldst thou bribe me—me, a brother of the Sacred Society of the Holy Jesus, Licentiate of Cordoba and Inquisitor of Guadalajara? Thinkest thou to buy me with thy sordid treasure? Avaunt!"

What might have been the issue of this rupture, and how complete might have been the triumph of the Holy Father over the Arch-Fiend, who was recoiling aghast at these sacred titles and the flourishing symbol, we can never know, for at that moment the crucifix slipped through his fingers.

Scarcely had it touched the ground before Devil and Holy Father simultaneously cast themselves toward it. In the struggle they clinched, and the pious José, who was as much the superior of his antagonist in bodily as in spiritual strength, was about to treat the Great Adversary to a back somersault, when he suddenly felt the long nails of the stranger piercing his flesh. A new fear seized his heart, a numbing chillness crept through his body, and he struggled to free himself, but in vain. A strange roaring was in his ears; the lake and cavern danced before his eyes and vanished; and with a loud cry he sank senseless to the ground.

When he recovered his consciousness he was aware of a gentle swaying motion of his body. He opened his eyes, and saw it was high noon, and that he was being carried in a litter through the valley. He felt stiff, and, looking down, perceived that his arm was tightly bandaged to his side.

He closed his eyes and after a few words of thankful prayer, thought how miraculously he had been preserved, and made a vow of candlesticks to the blessed Saint José. He then called in a faint voice, and presently the penitent Ignacio stood beside him.

The joy the poor fellow felt at his patron's returning consciousness for some time choked his utterance. He could only ejaculate, "A miracle! Blessed Saint José, he lives!" and kiss the Padre's bandaged hand. Father José, more intent on his last night's experience, waited for his emotion to subside, and asked where he had been found.

"On the mountain, your Reverence, but a few varas from where he attacked you."

"How?—You saw him then?" asked the Padre, in unfeigned astonishment.

"Saw him, your Reverence! Mother of God, I should think I did! And your Reverence shall see him too, if he ever comes again within range of Ignacio's arquebuse."

"What mean you, Ignacio?" said the Padre, sitting bolt-upright in his litter.

"Why, the bear, your Reverence—the bear, Holy Father, who attacked your worshipful person while you were meditating on the top of yonder mountain."

"Ah!" said the Holy Father, lying down again. "Chut, child! I would be at peace."

When he reached the Mission, he was tenderly cared for, and in a few weeks was enabled to resume those duties from which, as will be seen, not even the machinations of the Evil One could divert him. The news of his physical disaster spread over the country; and a letter to the Bishop of Guadalajara contained a confidential and detailed account of the good Father's spiritual temptation. But in some way the story leaked out; and long after José was gathered to his fathers, his mysterious encounter formed the theme of thrilling and whispered narrative. The mountain was generally shunned. It is true that Señor Joaquin Pedrillo afterward located a grant near the base of the mountain;

but as Señora Pedrillo was known to be a termagant half-breed, the Señor was not supposed to be over-fastidious.

Such is the Legend of Monte del Diablo. As I said before, it may seem to lack essential corroboration. The discrepancy between the Father's narrative and the actual climax has given rise to some skepticism on the part of ingenious quibblers. All such I would simply refer to that part of the report of Señor Julio Serro, Sub-Prefect of San Pablo, before whom attest of the above was made. Touching this matter, the worthy Prefect observes, "That although the body of Father José doth show evidence of grievous conflict in the flesh, yet that is no proof that the Enemy of Souls, who could assume the figure of a decorous elderly caballero, could not at the same time transform himself into a bear for his own vile purposes."

WAN LEE, THE PAGAN

As I opened Hop Sing's letter, there fluttered to the ground a square strip of yellow paper covered with hieroglyphics, which, at first glance, I innocently took to be the label from a pack of Chinese firecrackers. But the same envelope also contained a smaller strip of rice paper, with two Chinese characters traced in India ink, that I at once knew to be Hop Sing's visiting card. The whole, as afterwards literally translated, ran as follows:

TO THE STRANGER THE GATES OF MY HOUSE ARE NOT CLOSED; THE RICE JAR IS ON THE LEFT, AND THE SWEETMEATS ON THE RIGHT, AS YOU ENTER.

TWO SAYINGS OF THE MASTER:

HOSPITALITY IS THE VIRTUE OF THE SON AND THE WISDOM OF THE ANCESTOR.

THE SUPERIOR MAN IS LIGHT HEARTED AFTER THE CROP GATHERING; HE MAKES A FESTIVAL.

WHEN THE STRANGER IS IN YOUR MELON PATCH, OBSERVE HIM NOT TOO CLOSELY: INATTENTION IS OFTEN THE HIGHEST FORM OF CIVILITY.

HAPPINESS, PEACE, AND PROSPERITY.
HOP SING

WAN LEE, THE PAGAN

Admirable, certainly, as was this morality and pro-
verbial wisdom, and although this last axiom was very
characteristic of my friend Hop Sing, who was that
most somber of all humorists, a Chinese philosopher,
I must confess, that, even after a very free translation, I
was at a loss to make any immediate application of the
message. Luckily I discovered a third enclosure in the
shape of a little note in English, and Hop Sing's own
commercial hand. It ran thus:

THE PLEASURE OF YOUR COMPANY IS REQUESTED AT NO. —
SACRAMENTO STREET, ON FRIDAY EVENING AT EIGHT O'CLOCK. A
CUP OF TEA AT NINE SHARP.

HOP SING

This explained all. It meant a visit to Hop Sing's
warehouse, the opening and exhibition of some rare
Chinese novelties and curios, a chat in the back office,
a cup of tea of a perfection unknown beyond these
sacred precincts, cigars, and a visit to the Chinese
theater or temple. This was, in fact, the favorite pro-
gram of Hop Sing when he exercised his functions of
hospitality as the chief factor or superintendent of the
Ning Foo Company.

At eight o'clock on Friday evening, I entered the
warehouse of Hop Sing. There was that deliciously
commingled mysterious foreign odor that I had so often
noticed; there was the old array of uncouth-looking

137

objects, the long procession of jars and crockery, the same singular blending of the grotesque and the mathematically neat and exact, the same endless suggestions of frivolity and fragility, the same want of harmony in colors, that were each, in themselves, beautiful and rare. Kites in the shape of enormous dragons and gigantic butterflies; kites so ingeniously arranged as to utter at intervals, when facing the wind, the cry of a hawk; kites so large as to be beyond any boy's power of restraint—so large that you understood why kite flying in China was an amusement for adults; gods of china and bronze so gratuitously ugly as to be beyond any human interest or sympathy from their very impossibility; jars of sweetmeats covered all over with moral sentiments from Confucius; hats that looked like baskets, and baskets that looked like hats; silks so light that I hesitate to record the incredible number of square yards that you might pass through the ring on your little finger—these, and a great many other indescribable objects, were all familiar to me. I pushed my way through the dimly-lighted warehouse, until I reached the back office, or parlor, where I found Hop Sing waiting to receive me.

Before I describe him, I want the average reader to discharge from his mind any idea of a Chinaman that he may have gathered from the pantomime. He did not wear beautifully scalloped drawers fringed with little bells (I never met a Chinaman who did); he did not habitually carry his forefinger extended before him at right angles with his body; nor did I ever hear him utter the mysterious sentence, "Ching a ring a ring chaw;" nor dance under any provocation. He was, on the whole, a rather grave, decorous, handsome gentleman. His complexion, which extended all over his head, except where his long pig-tail grew, was like a very nice piece of glazed brown paper muslin. His eyes were black and bright, and his eyelids set at an angle of fifteen degrees; his nose straight, and delicately formed; his mouth small; and his teeth white and clean. He wore a dark blue silk blouse; and in the streets, on cold days, a short jacket of astrakhan fur. He wore, also, a pair of drawers of blue brocade gathered tightly over his calves and ankles, offering a general sort of suggestion, that he had forgotten his trousers that morning, but that, so gentlemanly were his manners, his friends had forborne to mention the fact to him. His manner was urbane, although quite serious. He spoke French and English fluently. In brief, I doubt if you could have found the equal of this Pagan shopkeeper among the Christian traders of San Francisco.

139

There were a few others present: a judge of the federal court, an editor, a high government official, and a prominent merchant. After we had drunk our tea, and tasted a few sweetmeats from a mysterious jar, that looked as if it might contain a preserved mouse among its other nondescript treasures, Hop Sing arose, and, gravely beckoning us to follow him, began to descend to the basement. When we got there, we were amazed at finding it brilliantly lighted, and that a number of chairs were arranged in a half-circle on the asphalt pavement. When he had courteously seated us, he said:

"I have invited you to witness a performance which I can at least promise you no other foreigners but yourselves have ever seen. Wang, the court-juggler, arrived here yesterday morning. He has never given a performance outside of the palace before. I have asked him to entertain my friends this evening. He requires no theater, stage accessories, or any confederate— nothing more than you see here. Will you be pleased to examine the ground yourselves, gentlemen."

Of course we examined the premises. It was the ordinary basement or cellar of the San Francisco storehouse, cemented to keep out the damp. We poked our sticks into the pavement, and rapped on the walls, to satisfy our polite host—but for no other purpose. We were quite content to be the victims of any clever deception. For myself, I knew I was ready to be deluded to any extent, and, if I had been offered an explanation of what followed, I should have probably declined it.

Although I am satisfied that Wang's general performance was the first of that kind ever given on American soil, it has, probably, since become so familiar to many of my readers, that I shall not bore them with it here. He began by setting to flight, with the aid of his fan, the usual number of butterflies, made before our eyes of little bits of tissue-paper, and kept them in the air during the remainder of the performance. I have a vivid recollection of the judge trying to catch one that had lit on his knee, and of its evading him with the pertinacity of a living insect. And, even at this time, Wang, still plying his fan, was taking chickens out of hats, making oranges disappear, pulling endless yards of silk from his sleeve, apparently filling the whole area of the basement with goods that appeared mysteriously from the ground, from his own sleeves, from nowhere! He swallowed knives to the ruin of his digestion for years to come; he dislocated every limb of his body; he reclined in the air, apparently upon nothing. But his crowning performance, which I have never yet seen repeated, was the most weird, mysterious, and astounding. It is my apology for this long introduction, my sole excuse for writing this article, and the genesis of this veracious history.

He cleared the ground of its encumbering articles for a space of about fifteen feet square, and then invited us all to walk forward, and again examine it. We did so gravely. There was nothing but the cemented pavement below to be seen or felt. He then asked for the loan of a handkerchief; and, as I chanced to be nearest him, I offered mine. He took it, and spread it open upon the floor. Over this he spread a large square of silk, and over this, again, a large shawl nearly covering the space he had cleared. He then took a position at one of the points of this rectangle, and began a monotonous chant, rocking his body to and fro in time with the somewhat lugubrious air.

We sat still and waited. Above the chant we could hear the striking of the city clocks, and the occasional rattle of a cart in the street overhead. The absolute watchfulness and expectation, the dim, mysterious half light of the cellar falling in a gruesome way upon the misshapen bulk of a Chinese deity in the back ground, a faint smell of opium-smoke mingling with spice, and the dreadful uncertainty of what we were really waiting for, sent an uncomfortable thrill down our backs, and made us look at each other with a forced and unnatural smile. This feeling was heightened when Hop Sing slowly rose, and, without a word, pointed with his finger to the center of the shawl.

There was something beneath the shawl. Surely— and something that was not there before; at first a mere suggestion in relief, a faint outline, but growing more and more distinct and visible every moment. The chant still continued; the perspiration began to roll from the singer's face; gradually the hidden object took upon itself a shape and bulk that raised the shawl in its center some five or six inches. It was now unmistakably the outline of a small but perfect human figure, with extended arms and legs. One or two of us turned pale. There was a feeling of general uneasiness, until the editor broke the silence by a gibe, that, poor as it was, was received with spontaneous enthusiasm. Then the chant suddenly ceased. Wang arose, and with a quick, dexterous movement, stripped both shawl and silk away, and discovered, sleeping peacefully upon my handkerchief, a tiny Chinese baby.

The applause and uproar which followed this revelation ought to have satisfied Wang, even if his audience was a small one: it was loud enough to awaken the baby—a pretty little boy about a year old, looking like a Cupid cut out of sandalwood. He was whisked away almost as mysteriously as he appeared. When Hop Sing returned my handkerchief to me with a bow, I asked if the juggler was the father of the baby. "No sabe!" said the imperturbable Hop Sing, taking refuge in that Spanish form of non-committalism so common in California.

"But does he have a new baby for every performance?" I asked.

"Perhaps. Who knows?"

"But what will become of this one?"

"Whatever you choose, gentlemen," replied Hop Sing with a courteous inclination. "It was born here: you are its godfathers."

There were two characteristic peculiarities of any Californian assemblage in 1856: it was quick to take a hint, and generous to the point of prodigality in its response to any charitable appeal. No matter how sordid or avaricious the individual, he could not resist the infection of sympathy. I doubled the points of my handkerchief into a bag, dropped a coin into it, and, without a word, passed it to the judge. He quietly added a twenty-dollar gold-piece, and passed it to the next. When it was returned to me, it contained over a hundred dollars. I knotted the money in the handkerchief, and gave it to Hop Sing.

"For the baby, from its godfathers."

"But what name?" said the judge. There was a running fire of "Erebus," "Nox," "Plutus," "Terra Cotta,"

"Antaeus," etcetera. Finally the question was referred to our host.

"Why not keep his own name?" he said quietly. "Wan Lee." And he did.

And thus was Wan Lee, on the night of Friday, the 5th of March, 1856, born into this veracious chronicle.

The last form of the *Northern Star* for the 19th of July, 1865—the only daily paper published in Klamath County—had just gone to press; and at three a.m., I was putting aside my proofs and manuscripts, preparatory to going home, when I discovered a letter lying under some sheets of paper, which I must have overlooked. The envelope was considerably soiled: it had no post-mark; but I had no difficulty in recognizing the hand of my friend Hop Sing. I opened it hurriedly, and read as follows:

MY DEAR SIR,

I DO NOT KNOW WHETHER THE BEARER WILL SUIT YOU; BUT, UNLESS THE OFFICE OF 'DEVIL' IN YOUR NEWSPAPER IS A PURELY TECHNICAL ONE, I THINK HE HAS ALL THE QUALITIES REQUIRED. HE IS VERY QUICK, ACTIVE, AND INTELLIGENT; UNDERSTANDS ENGLISH BETTER THAN HE SPEAKS IT; AND MAKES UP FOR ANY DEFECT BY HIS HABITS OF OBSERVATION AND IMITATION. YOU HAVE ONLY TO SHOW HIM HOW TO DO A THING ONCE, AND HE WILL REPEAT IT, WHETHER IT IS AN OFFENSE OR A VIRTUE. BUT YOU CERTAINLY KNOW HIM ALREADY. YOU ARE ONE OF HIS GODFATHERS; FOR IS HE NOT WAN LEE, THE REPUTED SON OF WANG THE CONJURER, TO WHOSE PERFORMANCES

I HAD THE HONOR TO INTRODUCE YOU? BUT PERHAPS YOU HAVE FORGOTTEN IT.

I SHALL SEND HIM WITH A GANG OF COOLIES TO STOCKTON, THENCE BY EXPRESS TO YOUR TOWN. IF YOU CAN USE HIM THERE, YOU WILL DO ME A FAVOR, AND PROBABLY SAVE HIS LIFE, WHICH IS AT PRESENT IN GREAT PERIL FROM THE HANDS OF THE YOUNGER MEMBERS OF YOUR CHRISTIAN AND HIGHLY-CIVILIZED RACE WHO ATTEND THE ENLIGHTENED SCHOOLS IN SAN FRANCISCO.

HE HAS ACQUIRED SOME SINGULAR HABITS AND CUSTOMS FROM HIS EXPERIENCE OF WANG'S PROFESSION, WHICH HE FOLLOWED FOR SOME YEARS, UNTIL HE BECAME TOO LARGE TO GO IN A HAT, OR BE PRODUCED FROM HIS FATHER'S SLEEVE. THE MONEY YOU LEFT WITH ME HAS BEEN EXPENDED ON HIS EDUCATION. HE HAS GONE THROUGH THE TRI-LITERAL CLASSICS, BUT, I THINK, WITHOUT MUCH BENEFIT. HE KNOWS BUT LITTLE OF CONFUCIUS, AND ABSOLUTELY NOTHING OF MENCIUS. OWING TO THE NEGLIGENCE OF HIS FATHER, HE ASSOCIATED, PERHAPS, TOO MUCH WITH AMERICAN CHILDREN.

I SHOULD HAVE ANSWERED YOUR LETTER BEFORE, BY POST; BUT I THOUGHT THAT WAN LEE HIMSELF WOULD BE A BETTER MESSENGER FOR THIS.

YOURS RESPECTFULLY,

HOP SING

And this was the long-delayed answer to my letter to Hop Sing. But where was the bearer? How was the letter delivered? I summoned hastily the foreman, printers, and office boy, but without eliciting anything. No one had seen the letter delivered, nor knew any thing of the bearer. A few days later, I had a visit from my laundryman, Ah Ri.

"You wantee debbil? All lightee. Me catchee him."

He returned in a few moments with a bright-looking Chinese boy, about ten years old, with whose appearance and general intelligence I was so greatly impressed, that I engaged him on the spot. When the business was concluded, I asked his name.

"Wan Lee," said the boy.

"What! Are you the boy sent out by Hop Sing? What the devil do you mean by not coming here before? and how did you deliver that letter?"

Wan Lee looked at me, and laughed. "Me pitchee in top side window."

I did not understand. He looked for a moment perplexed, and then, snatching the letter out of my hand, ran down the stairs. After a moment's pause, to my great astonishment, the letter came flying in the window, circled twice around the room, and then dropped gently, like a bird upon my table. Before I had got over my surprise, Wan Lee reappeared, smiled, looked at the letter and then at me, said, "So, John," and then remained gravely silent. I said nothing further; but it was understood that this was his first official act.

His next performance, I grieve to say, was not attended with equal success. One of our regular paper carriers fell sick, and, at a pinch, Wan Lee was ordered to fill his place. To prevent mistakes, he was shown over the route the previous evening, and supplied at about daylight with the usual number of subscribers' copies. He returned, after an hour, in good spirits, and without the papers. He had delivered them all, he said.

Unfortunately for Wan Lee, at about eight o'clock, indignant subscribers began to arrive at the office. They had received their copies; but how? In the form of hard-pressed cannonballs, delivered by a single shot, and a mere tour de force, through the glass of bedroom-windows. They had received them full in the face, like a base ball, if they happened to be up and stirring; they had received them in quarter sheets, tucked in at separate windows; they had found them in the chimney, pinned against the door, shot through attic windows, delivered in long slips through convenient keyholes, stuffed into ventilators, and occupying the same can with the morning's milk. One subscriber, who waited for some time at the office door to have a personal interview with Wan Lee (then comfortably locked in my bedroom), told me, with tears of rage in his eyes, that he had been awakened at five o'clock by a most hideous yelling below his windows; that, on rising in great agitation, he was startled by the sudden appearance of the *Northern Star,* rolled hard, and bent into the form of a boomerang, or East Indian club, that sailed into the window, described a number of fiendish circles in the room, knocked over the light, slapped the baby's face, took him (the subscriber) in the jaw, and then returned out of the window, and dropped helplessly in the area. During the rest of the day, wads and strips of soiled paper, purporting to be copies of the *Northern Star* of that morning's issue, were brought indignantly to the office. An admirable editorial on "The Resources of Humboldt County," which I had constructed the evening before, and which, I had reason to believe, might have changed the whole balance of trade during the ensuing year, and left San Francisco bankrupt at her wharves, was in this way lost to the public.

It was deemed advisable for the next three weeks to keep Wan Lee closely confined to the printing office and the purely mechanical part of the business. Here he developed a surprising quickness and adaptability, winning even the favor and good will of the printers and foreman, who at first looked upon his introduction into the secrets of their trade as fraught with the gravest political significance. He learned to set type readily and neatly, his wonderful skill in manipulation aiding him in the mere mechanical act, and his ignorance of the language confining him simply to the mechanical effort, confirming the printer's axiom, that the printer who considers or follows the ideas of his copy makes a poor compositor. He would set up deliberately long diatribes against himself, composed by his fellow-printers, and hung on his hook as copy, and even such short sentences as "Wan Lee is the devil's own imp," "Wan Lee is a Mongolian rascal," and bring the proof to me with happiness beaming from every tooth, and satisfaction shining in his huckleberry eyes.

It was not long, however, before he learned to retaliate on his mischievous persecutors. I remember one instance in which his reprisal came very near involving me in a serious misunderstanding. Our foreman's name was Webster; and Wan Lee presently learned to know and recognize the individual and combined letters of his name. It was during a political campaign; and the eloquent and fiery Col. Starbottle of Siskyou had delivered an effective speech, which was reported especially for the *Northern Star.* In a very sublime peroration, Col. Starbottle had said, "In the language of the godlike Webster, I repeat"—and here followed the quotation, which I have forgotten. Now, it chanced that Wan Lee, looking over the galley after it had been revised, saw the name of his chief persecutor, and, of course, imagined the quotation his. After the form was locked up, Wan Lee took advantage of Webster's absence to remove the quotation, and substitute a thin piece of lead, of the same size as the type, engraved with Chinese characters, making a sentence, which, I had reason to believe, was an utter and abject confession of the incapacity and offensiveness of the Webster family generally, and exceedingly eulogistic of Wan Lee himself personally.

The next morning's paper contained Col. Starbottle's speech in full, in which it appeared that the godlike Webster had, on one occasion, uttered his thoughts in excellent but perfectly enigmatical Chinese. The rage of Col. Starbottle knew no bounds. I have a vivid recollection of that admirable man walking into my office, and demanding a retraction of the statement.

"But my dear sir," I asked, "are you willing to deny, over your own signature, that Webster ever uttered such a sentence? Dare you deny, that, with Mr. Webster's well-known attainments, a knowledge of Chinese might not have been among the number? Are you willing to submit a translation suitable to the capacity of our readers, and deny, upon your honor as a gentleman, that the late Mr. Webster ever uttered such a sentiment? If you are, sir, I am willing to publish your denial."

The colonel was not, and left, highly indignant.

Webster, the foreman, took it more coolly. Happily, he was unaware, that, for two days after, Chinamen from the laundries, from the gulches, from the kitchens, looked in the front office door, with faces beaming with sardonic delight; that three hundred extra copies of the "Star" were ordered for the wash houses on the river. He only knew, that, during the day, Wan Lee occasionally went off into convulsive spasms, and that he was obliged to kick him into consciousness again. A week after the occurrence, I called Wan Lee into my office.

"Wan," I said gravely, "I should like you to give me, for my own personal satisfaction, a translation of that Chinese sentence which my gifted countryman, the late godlike Webster, uttered upon a public occasion." Wan Lee looked at me intently, and then the slightest possible twinkle crept into his black eyes. Then he replied with equal gravity:

"Mishtel Webstel, he say, 'China boy makee me belly much foolee. China boy makee me heap sick.'" Which I have reason to think was true.

But I fear I am giving but one side, and not the best, of Wan Lee's character. As he imparted it to me, his had been a hard life. He had known scarcely any childhood: he had no recollection of a father or mother. The conjurer Wang had brought him up. He had spent the first seven years of his life in appearing from baskets, in dropping out of hats, in climbing ladders, in putting his little limbs out of joint in posturing. He had lived in an atmosphere of trickery and deception. He had learned to look upon mankind as dupes of their senses: in fine, if he had thought at all, he would have been a skeptic; if he had been a little older, he would have been a cynic; if he had been older still, he would have been a philosopher. As it was, he was a little imp. A good-natured imp it was, too—an imp whose moral nature had never been awakened—an imp up for a holiday, and willing to try virtue as a diversion. I don't know that he had any spiritual nature. He was very superstitious. He carried about with him a hideous little porcelain god, which he was in the habit of alternately reviling and propitiating. He was too intelligent for the commoner Chinese vices of stealing or gratuitous lying. Whatever discipline he practiced was taught by his intellect.

I am inclined to think that his feelings were not altogether unimpressible, although it was almost impossible to extract an expression from him; and I conscientiously believe he became attached to those that were good to him. What he might have become under more favorable conditions than the bondsman of an overworked, underpaid literary man, I don't know. I only know that the scant, irregular, impulsive kindnesses that I showed him were gratefully received. He was very loyal and patient, two qualities rare in the average American servant. He was like Malvolio, "sad and civil" with me. Only once, and then under great provocation, do I remember of his exhibiting any impatience. It was my habit, after leaving the office at night, to take him with me to my rooms, as the bearer of any supplemental or happy afterthought, in the editorial way, that might occur to me before the paper went to press. One night I had been scribbling away past the usual hour of dismissing Wan Lee, and had become quite oblivious of his presence in a chair near my door, when suddenly I became aware of a voice saying in plaintive accents, something that sounded like "Chy Lee."

I faced around sternly.

"What did you say?"

"Me say, 'Chy Lee.'"

"Well?" I said impatiently.

"You sabe, 'How do, John'?"

"Yes."

"You sabe, 'So long, John'?"

"Yes."

"Well, 'Chy Lee' allee same!"

I understood him quite plainly. It appeared that "Chy Lee" was a form of "good night," and that Wan Lee was anxious to go home. But an instinct of mischief, which, I fear, I possessed in common with him, impelled me to act as if oblivious of the hint. I muttered something about not understanding him, and again bent over my work. In a few minutes I heard his wooden shoes pattering pathetically over the floor. I looked up. He was standing near the door.

"You no sabe, 'Chy Lee'?"

"No," I said sternly.

"You sabe muchee big foolee! allee same!"

And, with this audacity upon his lips, he fled. The next morning, however, he was as meek and patient as before, and I did not recall his offense. As a probable peace offering, he blacked all my boots—a duty never required of him—including a pair of buff deerskin slippers and an immense pair of horseman's jackboots, on which he indulged his remorse for two hours.

I have spoken of his honesty as being a quality of his intellect rather than his principle, but I recall about this time two exceptions to the rule. I was anxious to get some fresh eggs as a change to the heavy diet of a mining town; and, knowing that Wan Lee's country-men were great poultry raisers, I applied to him. He furnished me with them regularly every morning, but refused to take any pay, saying that the man did not sell them, a remarkable instance of self-abnegation, as eggs were then worth half a dollar apiece. One morn-ing my neighbor Forster dropped in upon me at breakfast, and took occasion to bewail his own ill fortune, as his hens had lately stopped laying, or wandered off in the bush. Wan Lee, who was present during our colloquy, preserved his characteristic sad taciturnity. When my neighbor had gone, he turned to me with a slight chuckle: "Flostel's hens—Wan Lee's hens allee same!" His other offense was more serious and ambitious. It was a season of great irregularities in the mails, and Wan Lee had heard me deplore the delay in the delivery of my letters and newspapers. On arriving at my office one day, I was amazed to find my table covered with letters, evidently just from the post office, but, unfortunately, not one addressed to me. I turned to Wan Lee, who was surveying them with a calm satisfaction, and demanded an explanation. To my horror he pointed to an empty mailbag in the corner, and said, "Postman he say, 'No lettee, John; no lettee, John.' Postman plentee lie! Postman no good. Me catchee lettee last night allee same!" Luckily it was still early: the mails had not been distributed. I had a hurried interview with the postmaster; and Wan Lee's bold attempt at robbing the United States mail was finally condoned by the purchase of a new mailbag, and the whole affair thus kept a secret.

If my liking for my little Pagan page had not been sufficient, my duty to Hop Sing was enough, to cause me to take Wan Lee with me when I returned to San

Francisco after my two years' experience with the *Northern Star.* I do not think he contemplated the change with pleasure. I attributed his feelings to a nervous dread of crowded public streets (when he had to go across town for me on an errand, he always made a circuit of the outskirts), to his dislike for the discipline of the Chinese and English school to which I proposed to send him, to his fondness for the free, vagrant life of the mines, to sheer willfulness. That it might have been a superstitious premonition did not occur to me until long after.

Nevertheless it really seemed as if the opportunity I had long looked for and confidently expected had come—the opportunity of placing Wan Lee under gently restraining influences, of subjecting him to a life and experience that would draw out of him what good my superficial care and ill-regulated kindness could not reach. Wan Lee was placed at the school of a Chinese missionary, an intelligent and kind-hearted clergyman, who had shown great interest in the boy, and who, better than all, had a wonderful faith in him. A home was found for him in the family of a widow, who had a bright and interesting daughter about two years younger than Wan Lee. It was this bright, cheery, innocent, and artless child that touched and reached a depth in the boy's nature that hitherto had been unsuspected; that awakened a moral susceptibility which had lain for years insensible alike to the teachings of society, or the ethics of the theologian.

These few brief months—bright with a promise that we never saw fulfilled—must have been happy ones to Wan Lee. He worshipped his little friend with something of the same superstition, but without any of the caprice, that he bestowed upon his porcelain pagan god. It was his delight to walk behind her to school, carrying her books—a service always fraught with danger to him from the little hands of his Caucasian Christian brothers. He made her the most marvelous toys; he would cut out of carrots and turnips the most astonishing roses and tulips; he made life-like chickens out of melon seeds; he constructed fans and kites, and was singularly proficient in the making of dolls' paper dresses. On the other hand, she played and sang to him, taught him a thousand little prettinesses and refinements only known to girls, gave him a yellow ribbon for his pig-tail, as best suiting his complexion, read to him, showed him wherein he was original and valuable, took him to Sunday school with her, against the precedents of the school, and, small-womanlike, triumphed. I wish I could add here, that she effected his conversion, and made him give up his porcelain idol. But I am telling a true story; and this little girl was quite content to fill him with her own Christian goodness, without letting him know that he was changed. So they got along very well together—this little Christian girl with her shining cross hanging around her plump, white little neck; and this dark little pagan, with his hideous porcelain god hidden away in his blouse.

There were two days of that eventful year which will long be remembered in San Francisco—two days when a mob of her citizens set upon and killed unarmed, defenseless foreigners because they were foreigners, and of another race, religion, and color, and worked for what wages they could get. There were some public men so timid, that, seeing this, they thought that the end of the world had come. There were some eminent statesmen, whose names I am ashamed to write here, who began to think that the passage in the Constitution which guarantees civil and religious liberty to every citizen or foreigner was a mistake. But there were, also, some men who were not so easily frightened; and in twenty-four hours we had things so arranged, that the timid men could wring their hands in safety, and the eminent statesmen utter their doubts without hurting anybody or anything. And in the midst of this I got a note from Hop Sing, asking me to come to him immediately.

I found his warehouse closed, and strongly guarded by the police against any possible attack of the rioters. Hop Sing admitted me through a barred grating with his usual imperturbable calm, but, as it seemed to me, with more than his usual seriousness. Without a word, he took my hand, and led me to the rear of the room, and thence down stairs into the basement. It was dimly lighted; but there was something lying on the floor covered by a shawl. As I approached he drew the shawl away with a sudden gesture and revealed Wan Lee, the pagan, lying there dead.

Dead, my reverend friends, dead—stoned to death in the streets of San Francisco, in the year of grace 1869, by a mob of half-grown boys and Christian school-children!

As I put my hand reverently upon his breast, I felt something crumbling beneath his blouse. I looked inquiringly at Hop Sing. He put his hand between the folds of silk, and drew out something with the first bitter smile I had ever seen on the face of that Pagan gentleman.

It was Wan Lee's porcelain god, crushed by a stone from the hands of those Christian iconoclasts!

AN INGENUE OF THE SIERRAS

I.

We all held our breath as the coach rushed through the semi-darkness of Galloper's Ridge. The vehicle itself was only a huge lumbering shadow; its sidelights were carefully extinguished, and Yuba Bill had just politely removed from the lips of an out-side passenger even the cigar with which he had been ostentatiously exhibiting his coolness. For it had been rumored that the Ramon Martinez gang of road agents were laying for us on the second grade, and would time the passage of our lights across Galloper's in order to intercept us in the brush beyond. If we could cross the ridge without being seen, and so get through the brush before they reached it, we were safe. If they followed, it would only be a stern chase with the odds in our favor.

The huge vehicle swayed from side to side, rolled, dipped, and plunged, but Bill kept the track, as if, in the whispered words of the expressman, he could "feel and smell" the road he could no longer see. We knew that at times we hung perilously over the edge of slopes that eventually dropped a thousand feet sheer to the tops of the sugar pines below, but we knew that Bill knew it also. The half-visible heads of the horses, drawn wedgewise together by the tightened reins, appeared to cleave the darkness like a ploughshare, held between his rigid hands. Even the hoof beats of the six horses had fallen into a vague, monotonous, distant roll. Then the ridge was crossed, and we plunged into the still blacker obscurity of the brush. Rather we no longer seemed to move—it was only the phantom night that rushed by us. The horses might have been submerged in some swift Lethean stream; nothing but the top of the coach and the rigid bulk of Yuba Bill arose above them. Yet even in that awful moment our speed was unslackened; it was as if Bill cared no longer to *guide* but only to drive, or as if the direction of his huge machine was determined by other hands than his. An incautious whisperer hazarded the paralyzing suggestion of our meeting another team. To our great astonishment, Bill overheard it; to our greater astonishment, he replied. "It 'ud be only a neck and neck race which would get to hell first," he said quietly. But we were relieved—for he had *spoken!* Almost simultaneously the wider turnpike began to glimmer faintly as a visible track before us; the wayside trees fell out of line, opened up, and dropped off one after another; we were on the broader tableland, out of danger, and apparently unperceived and unpursued.

Nevertheless in the conversation that broke out again with the relighting of the lamps, and the comments, congratulations, and reminiscences that were freely exchanged, Yuba Bill preserved a dissatisfied and even resentful silence. The most generous praise of his skill and courage awoke no response. "I reckon the old man waz just spilin' for a fight, and is feelin' disappointed," said a passenger. But those who knew that Bill had the true fighter's scorn for any purely purposeless conflict were more or less concerned and watchful of him. He would drive steadily for four or five minutes with thoughtfully knitted brows, but eyes still keenly observant under his slouched hat, and then, relaxing his strained attitude, would give way to a movement of impatience. "You ain't uneasy about anything, Bill, are you?" asked the expressman confidentially. Bill lifted his eyes with a slightly contemptuous surprise. "Not about anything ter *come*. It's what *hez* happened that I don't exackly *sabe*. I don't see no signs of Ramon's gang ever havin' been out at all, and ef they were out I don't see why they didn't go for us."

"The simple fact is that our ruse was successful," said an outside passenger. "They waited to see our

163

lights on the ridge, and, not seeing them, missed us until we had passed. That's my opinion."

"You ain't puttin' any price on that opinion, air ye?" inquired Bill politely.

"No."

"'Cos thar's a comic paper in 'Frisco pays for them things, and I've seen worse things in it."

"Come off, Bill," retorted the passenger, slightly nettled by the tittering of his companions. "Then what did you put out the lights for?"

"Well," returned Bill grimly, "it mout have been because I didn't keer to hev you chaps blazin' away at the first bush you *thought* you saw move in your skeer, and bringin' down their fire on us."

The explanation, though unsatisfactory, was by no means an improbable one, and we thought it better to accept it with a laugh. Bill, however, resumed his abstracted manner.

"Who got in at the Summit?" he at last asked abruptly of the expressman.

"Derrick and Simpson of Cold Spring, and one of the Excelsior boys," responded the expressman.

"And that Pike County girl from Dow's Flat, with her bundles. Don't forget her," added the outside passenger ironically.

"Does anybody here know her?" continued Bill, ignoring the irony.

"You'd better ask Judge Thompson; he was mighty attentive to her; gettin' her a seat by the off window, and lookin' after her bundles and things."

"Gettin' her a seat by the *window?*" repeated Bill.

"Yes, she wanted to see everything, and wasn't afraid of the shooting."

"Yes," broke in a third passenger, "and he was so d—d civil that when she dropped her ring in the straw, he struck a match agin all your rules, you know, and held it for her to find it. And it was just as we were crossin' through the brush, too. I saw the hull thing through the window, for I was hanging over the wheels with my gun ready for action. And it wasn't no fault of Judge Thompson's if his d—d foolishness hadn't shown us up, and got us a shot from the gang."

Bill gave a short grunt, but drove steadily on without further comment or even turning his eyes to the speaker.

We were now not more than a mile from the station, at the crossroads where we were to change horses. The lights already glimmered in the distance, and there was a faint suggestion of the coming dawn on the summits of the ridge to the west. We had plunged into a belt of timber, when suddenly a horseman emerged at a sharp canter from a trail that seemed to be parallel with our own. We were all slightly startled; Yuba Bill alone preserving his moody calm.

"Hullo!" he said.

The stranger wheeled to our side as Bill slackened his speed. He seemed to be a packer or freight muleteer.

"Ye didn't get held up on the Divide?" continued Bill cheerfully.

"No," returned the packer, with a laugh; "*I* don't carry treasure. But I see you're all right, too. I saw you crossin' over Galloper's."

"*Saw* us?" said Bill sharply. "We had our lights out."

"Yes, but there was suthin' white—a handkerchief or woman's veil, I reckon—hangin' from the window. It was only a movin' spot agin the hillside, but ez I was lookin' out for ye I knew it was you by that. Good night!"

He cantered away. We tried to look at each other's faces, and at Bill's expression in the darkness, but he neither spoke nor stirred until he threw down the reins when we stopped before the station. The passengers quickly descended from the roof; the expressman was about to follow, but Bill plucked his sleeve.

"I'm goin' to take a look over this yer stage and these yer passengers with ye, afore we start."

"Why, what's up?"

"Well," said Bill, slowly disengaging himself from one of his enormous gloves, "when we waltzed down into the brush up there I saw a man, ez plain ez I see you, rise up from it. I thought our time had come and the band was goin' to play, when he sorter drew back, made a sign, and we just scooted past him."

"Well?"

"Well," said Bill, "it means that this yer coach was *passed through free* tonight."

"You don't object to *that,* surely? I think we were deucedly lucky."

Bill slowly drew off his other glove. "I've been riskin' my everlastin' life on this d—d line three times a week," he said with mock humility, "and I'm allus thankful for small mercies. *But,*" he added grimly, "when it comes down to being passed free by some pal of a hoss thief, and thet called a speshal Providence, *I ain't in it!* No, sir, I ain't in it!"

II.

It was with mixed emotions that the passengers heard that a delay of fifteen minutes to tighten certain screw bolts had been ordered by the autocratic Bill. Some were anxious to get their breakfast at Sugar

Pine, but others were not averse to linger for the day-light that promised greater safety on the road. The expressman, knowing the real cause of Bill's delay, was nevertheless at a loss to understand the object of it. The passengers were all well known; any idea of com-plicity with the road agents was wild and impossible, and, even if there was a confederate of the gang among them, he would have been more likely to precipitate a robbery than to check it. Again, the discovery of such a confederate—to whom they clearly owed their safety—and his arrest would have been quite against the Californian sense of justice, if not actually illegal. It seemed evident that Bill's quixotic sense of honor was leading him astray.

The station consisted of a stable, a wagon shed, and a building containing three rooms. The first was fitted up with bunks or sleeping berths for the em-ployees; the second was the kitchen; and the third and larger apartment was dining room or sitting room, and was used as general waiting room for the passengers. It was not a refreshment station, and there was no bar. But a mysterious command from the omnipotent Bill produced a demijohn of whiskey, with which he hospi-tably treated the company. The seductive influence of the liquor loosened the tongue of the gallant Judge Thompson. He admitted to having struck a match to enable the fair Pike Countian to find her ring, which, however, proved to have fallen in her lap. She was "a fine, healthy young woman—a type of the Far West, sir; in fact, quite a prairie blossom! Yet simple and guileless as a child." She was on her way to Marysville, he believed, "although she expected to meet friends— a friend, in fact—later on." It was her first visit to a large town—in fact, any civilized center—since she crossed the plains three years ago. Her girlish curiosity was quite touching, and her innocence irresistible. In fact, in a country whose tendency was to produce "frivolity and forwardness in young girls," he found her "a most interesting young person." She was even then out in the stable yard watching the horses being harnessed, "preferring to indulge a pardonable healthy young curiosity than to listen to the empty compliments of the younger passengers."

The figure which Bill saw thus engaged, without being otherwise distinguished, certainly seemed to justify the Judge's opinion. She appeared to be a well-matured country girl, whose frank gray eyes and large laughing mouth expressed a wholesome and abiding gratification in her life and surroundings. She was watching the replacing of luggage in the boot. A little feminine start, as one of her own parcels was thrown somewhat roughly on the roof, gave Bill his opportunity.

169

"Now there," he growled to the helper, "ye ain't carting stone! Look out, will yer! Some of your things, miss?" he added, with gruff courtesy, turning to her. "These yer trunks, for instance?"

She smiled a pleasant assent, and Bill, pushing aside the helper, seized a large square trunk in his arms. But from excess of zeal, or some other mischance, his foot slipped, and he came down heavily, striking the corner of the trunk on the ground and loosening its hinges and fastenings. It was a cheap, common-looking affair, but the accident discovered in its yawning lid a quantity of white, lace-edged feminine apparel of an apparently superior quality. The young lady uttered another cry and came quickly forward, but Bill was profuse in his apologies, himself girded the broken box with a strap, and declared his intention of having the company "make it good" to her with a new one. Then he casually accompanied her to the door of the waiting room, entered, made a place for her before the fire by simply lifting the nearest and most youthful passenger by the coat collar from the stool that he was occupying, and, having installed the lady in it, displaced another man who was standing before the chimney, and, drawing himself up to his full six feet of height in front of her, glanced down upon

170

his fair passenger as he took his waybill from his pocket.

"Your name is down here as Miss Mullins?" he said.

She looked up, became suddenly aware that she and her questioner were the center of interest to the whole circle of passengers, and, with a slight rise of color, returned, "Yes."

"Well, Miss Mullins, I've got a question or two to ask ye. I ask it straight out afore this crowd. It's in my rights to take ye aside and ask it—but that ain't my style; I'm no detective. I needn't ask it at all, but act as ef I knowed the answer, or I might leave it to be asked by others. Ye needn't answer it ef ye don't like; ye've got a friend over ther—Judge Thompson—who is a friend to ye, right or wrong, jest as any other man here is—as though ye'd packed your own jury. Well, the simple question I've got to ask ye is *this:* Did you signal to anybody from the coach when we passed Galloper's an hour ago?"

We all thought that Bill's courage and audacity had reached its climax here. To openly and publicly accuse a lady before a group of chivalrous Californians, and that lady possessing the further attractions of youth, good looks, and innocence, was little short of desperation. There was an evident movement of adhesion

171

towards the fair stranger, a slight muttering broke out on the right, but the very boldness of the act held them in stupefied surprise. Judge Thompson, with a bland propitiatory smile began: "Really, Bill, I must protest on behalf of this young lady"—when the fair accused, raising her eyes to her accuser, to the consternation of everybody answered with the slight but convincing hesitation of conscientious truthfulness:

"I did."

"Ahem!" interposed the Judge hastily, "er—that is—er—you allowed your handkerchief to flutter from the window—I noticed it myself—casually—one might say even playfully—but without any particular significance."

The girl, regarding her apologist with a singular mingling of pride and impatience, returned briefly:

"I signaled."

"Who did you signal to?" asked Bill gravely.

"The young gentleman I'm going to marry."

A start, followed by a slight titter from the younger passengers, was instantly suppressed by a savage glance from Bill.

"What did you signal to him for?" he continued.

"To tell him I was here, and that it was all right," returned the young girl, with a steadily rising pride and color.

"Wot was all right?" demanded Bill.

"That I wasn't followed, and that he could meet me on the road beyond Cass's Ridge Station." She hesitated a moment, and then, with a still greater pride, in which a youthful defiance was still mingled, said:

"I've run away from home to marry him. And I mean to! No one can stop me. Dad didn't like him just because he was poor, and dad's got money. Dad wanted me to marry a man I hate, and got a lot of dresses and things to bribe me."

"And you're taking them in your trunk to the other feller?" said Bill grimly.

"Yes, he's poor," returned the girl defiantly.

"Then your father's name is Mullins?" asked Bill.

"It's not Mullins. I—I—took that name," she hesitated, with her first exhibition of self-consciousness.

"Wot *is* his name?"

"Eli Hemmings."

A smile of relief and significance went round the circle. The fame of Eli or "Skinner" Hemmings, as a notorious miser and usurer, had passed even beyond Galloper's Ridge.

"The step that you're taking, Miss Mullins, I need not tell you, is one of great gravity," said Judge Thompson, with a certain paternal seriousness of manner, in which, however, we were glad to detect a glaring

173

affectation; "and I trust that you and your affianced have fully weighed it. Far be it from me to interfere with or question the natural affections of two young people, but may I ask you what you know of the—er— young gentleman for whom you are sacrificing so much, and, perhaps, imperiling your whole future? For instance, have you known him long?"

The slightly troubled air of trying to understand— not unlike the vague wonderment of childhood—with which Miss Mullins had received the beginning of this exordium, changed to a relieved smile of comprehension as she said quickly, "Oh yes, nearly a whole year."

"And," said the Judge, smiling, "has he a vocation—is he in business?"

"Oh yes," she returned; "he's a collector."

"A collector?"

"Yes; he collects bills, you know—money," she went on, with childish eagerness, "not for himself—*he* never has any money, poor Charley—but for his firm. It's dreadful hard work, too; keeps him out for days and nights, over bad roads and baddest weather. Sometimes, when he's stole over to the ranch just to see me, he's been so bad he could scarcely keep his seat in the saddle, much less stand. And he's got to take mighty big risks, too. Times the folks are cross with him and won't pay; once they shot him in the arm,

174

and he came to me, and I helped do it up for him. But he don't mind. He's real brave—jest as brave as he's good." There was such a wholesome ring of truth in this pretty praise that we were touched in sympathy with the speaker.

"What firm does he collect for?" asked the Judge gently.

"I don't know exactly—he won't tell me—but I think it's a Spanish firm. You see"—she took us all into her confidence with a sweeping smile of innocent yet half-mischievous artfulness—"I only know because I peeped over a letter he once got from his firm, telling him he must hustle up and be ready for the road the next day—but I think the name was Martinez—yes, Ramon Martinez."

In the dead silence that ensued—a silence so profound that we could hear the horses in the distant stable yard rattling their harness—one of the younger Excelsior boys burst into a hysteric laugh, but the fierce eye of Yuba Bill was down upon him, and seemed to instantly stiffen him into a silent, grinning mask. The young girl, however, took no note of it. Following out, with lover-like diffusiveness, the reminiscences thus awakened, she went on:

"Yes, it's mighty hard work, but he says it's all for me, and as soon as we're married he'll quit it. He might have quit it before, but he won't take no money of me, nor what I told him I could get out of dad! That ain't his style. He's mighty proud—if he is poor—is Charley. Why thar's all ma's money which she left me in the Savin's Bank that I wanted to draw out—for I had the right—and give it to him, but he wouldn't hear of it! Why, he wouldn't take one of the things I've got with me, if he knew it. And so he goes on ridin' and ridin', here and there and everywhere, and gettin' more and more played out and sad, and thin and pale as a spirit, and always so uneasy about his business, and startin' up at times when we're meetin' out in the South Woods or in the far clearin', and sayin': 'I must be goin' now, Polly,' and yet always tryin' to be chiffle and chipper afore me. Why he must have rid miles and miles to have watched for me thar in the brush at the foot of Galloper's tonight, jest to see if all was safe; and Lordy! I'd have given him the signal and showed a light if I'd died for it the next minit. There! That's what I know of Charley—that's what I'm running away from home for—that's what I'm running to him for, and I don't care who knows it! And I only wish I'd done it afore—and I would—if—if—if—he'd only *asked me!* There now!" She stopped, panted, and choked. Then one of the sudden transitions of youthful emotion overtook the eager, laughing face; it clouded up with the swift change of childhood, a lightning quiver of expression broke over it, and—then came the rain!

I think this simple act completed our utter demoralization! We smiled feebly at each other with that assumption of masculine superiority which is miserably conscious of its own helplessness at such moments. We looked out of the window, blew our noses, said: "Eh—what?" and "I say," vaguely to each other, and were greatly relieved, and yet apparently astonished, when Yuba Bill, who had turned his back upon the fair speaker, and was kicking the logs in the fireplace, suddenly swept down upon us and bundled us all into the road, leaving Miss Mullins alone. Then he walked aside with Judge Thompson for a few moments; returned to us, autocratically demanded of the party a complete reticence towards Miss Mullins on the subject matter under discussion, re-entered the station, reappeared with the young lady, suppressed a faint idiotic cheer which broke from us at the spectacle of her innocent face once more cleared and rosy, climbed the box, and in another moment we were under way.

"Then she don't know what her lover is yet?" asked the expressman eagerly.

"No."

"Are *you* certain it's one of the gang?"

177

"Can't say *for sure.* It mout be a young chap from Yolo who bucked agin the tiger[1] at Sacramento, got regularly cleaned out and busted, and joined the gang for a flier. They say thar was a new hand in that job over at Keeley's—and a mighty game one, too; and ez there was some buckshot onloaded that trip, he might hev got his share, and that would tally with what the girl said about his arm. See! Ef that's the man, I've heered he was the son of some big preacher in the States, and a college sharp to boot, who ran wild in 'Frisco, and played himself for all he was worth. They're the wust kind to kick when they once get a foot over the traces. For stiddy, comf'ble kempany," added Bill reflectively, "give *me* the son of a man that was *hanged!*"

"But what are you going to do about this?"

"That depends upon the feller who comes to meet her."

"But you ain't going to try to take him? That would be playing it pretty low down on them both."

"Keep your hair on, Jimmy! The Judge and me are only going to rastle with the sperrit of that gay young galoot, when he drops down for his girl—and exhort him pow'ful! Ef he allows he's convicted of sin and will

---

[1] Gambled at faro.

178

find the Lord, we'll marry him and the gal offhand at the next station, and the Judge will officiate himself for nothin'. We're goin' to have this yer elopement done on the square—and our waybill clean—you bet!"

"But you don't suppose he'll trust himself in your hands?"

"Polly will signal to him that it's all square."

"Ah!" said the expressman. Nevertheless in those few moments the men seemed to have exchanged dispositions. The expressman looked doubtfully, critically, and even cynically before him. Bill's face had relaxed, and something like a bland smile beamed across it, as he drove confidently and unhesitatingly forward.

Day, meantime, although full blown and radiant on the mountain summits around us, was yet nebulous and uncertain in the valleys into which we were plunging. Lights still glimmered in the cabins and few ranch buildings which began to indicate the thicker settlements. And the shadows were heaviest in a little copse, where a note from Judge Thompson in the coach was handed up to Yuba Bill, who at once slowly began to draw up his horses. The coach stopped finally near the junction of a small crossroad. At the same moment Miss Mullins slipped down from the vehicle, and, with a parting wave of her hand to the Judge, who had assisted her from the steps, tripped down the crossroad, and disappeared in its semi-obscurity. To our surprise the stage waited, Bill holding the reins listlessly in his hands. Five minutes passed—an eternity of expectation, and, as there was that in Yuba Bill's face which forbade idle questioning, an aching void of silence also! This was at last broken by a strange voice from the road:

"Go on we'll follow."

The coach started forward. Presently we heard the sound of other wheels behind us. We all craned our necks backward to get a view of the unknown, but by the growing light we could only see that we were followed at a distance by a buggy with two figures in it. Evidently Polly Mullins and her lover! We hoped that they would pass us. But the vehicle, although drawn by a fast horse, preserved its distance always, and it was plain that its driver had no desire to satisfy our curiosity. The expressman had recourse to Bill.

"Is it the man you thought of?" he asked eagerly.

"I reckon," said Bill briefly.

"But," continued the expressman, returning to his former skepticism, "what's to keep them both from levanting together now?"

Bill jerked his hand towards the boot with a grim smile.

"Their baggage."

180

"Oh!" said the expressman.

"Yes," continued Bill. "We'll hang on to that gal's little frills and fixin's until this yer job's settled, and the ceremony's over, jest as ef we waz her own father. And, what's more, young man," he added, suddenly turning to the expressman, *"you'll* express them trunks of hers *through to Sacramento* with your kempany's labels, and hand her the receipts and checks for them, so she *can get 'em there.* That'll keep *him* outer temptation and the reach o' the gang, until they get away among white men and civilization again. When your hoary-headed ole grandfather, or, to speak plainer, that partikler old whiskey soaker known as Yuba Bill, wot sits on this box," he continued, with a diabolical wink at the expressman, "waltzes in to pervide for a young couple jest startin' in life, thar's nothin' mean about his style, you bet. He fills the bill every time! Speshul Providences take a back seat when he's around."

When the station hotel and straggling settlement of Sugar Pine, now distinct and clear in the growing light, at last rose within rifle shot on the plateau, the buggy suddenly darted swiftly by us, so swiftly that the faces of the two occupants were barely distinguishable as they passed, and keeping the lead by a dozen lengths, reached the door of the hotel. The young girl and her companion leaped down and vanished within as we drew up. They had evidently determined to elude our curiosity, and were successful.

But the material appetites of the passengers, sharpened by the keen mountain air, were more potent than their curiosity, and, as the breakfast bell rang out at the moment the stage stopped, a majority of them rushed into the dining room and scrambled for places without giving much heed to the vanished couple or to the Judge and Yuba Bill, who had disappeared also. The through coach to Marysville and Sacramento was likewise waiting, for Sugar Pine was the limit of Bill's ministration, and the coach which we had just left went no farther. In the course of twenty minutes, however, there was a slight and somewhat ceremonious bustling in the hall and on the veranda, and Yuba Bill and the Judge reappeared. The latter was leading, with some elaboration of manner and detail, the shapely figure of Miss Mullins, and Yuba Bill was accompanying her companion to the buggy. We all rushed to the windows to get a good view of the mysterious stranger and probable ex-brigand whose life was now linked with our fair fellow passenger. I am afraid, however, that we all participated in a certain impression of disappointment and doubt. Handsome and even cultivated-looking, he assuredly was—young and vigorous in appearance. But there was a certain half-shamed, half-defiant suggestion in his expression, yet coupled with a watchful lurking uneasiness which was not pleasant and hardly becoming in a bridegroom—and the possessor of such a bride. But the frank, joyous, innocent face of Polly Mullins, resplendent with a simple, happy confidence, melted our hearts again, and condoned the fellow's shortcomings. We waved our hands; I think we would have given three rousing cheers as they drove away if the omnipotent eye of Yuba Bill had not been upon us. It was well, for the next moment we were summoned to the presence of that soft-hearted autocrat.

We found him alone with the Judge in a private sitting-room, standing before a table on which there was a decanter and glasses. As we filed expectantly into the room and the door closed behind us, he cast a glance of hesitating tolerance over the group.

"Gentlemen," he said slowly, "you was all present at the beginnin' of a little game this mornin', and the judge thar thinks that you oughter be let in at the finish. *I* don't see that it's any of *your* d—d business—so to speak; but ez the Judge here allows you're all in the secret, I've called you in to take a partin' drink to the health of Mr. and Mrs. Charley Byng—ez is now comf'ably off on their bridal tower. What *you* know or what *you* suspects of the young galoot that's married

183

the gal ain't worth shucks to anybody, and I wouldn't give it to a yaller pup to play with, but the Judge thinks you ought all to promise right here that you'll keep it dark. That's his opinion. Ez far as my opinion goes, gen'l'men," continued Bill, with greater blandness and apparent cordiality, "I wanter simply remark, in a keerless, offhand gin'ral way, that ef I ketch any godforsaken, lop-eared, chuckle-headed blatherin' idjet airin' *his* opinion—"

"One moment, Bill," interposed Judge Thompson with a grave smile. "Let me explain. You understand, gentlemen," he said, turning to us, "the singular, and I may say affecting, situation which our good-hearted friend here has done so much to bring to what we hope will be a happy termination. I want to give here, as my professional opinion, that there is nothing in his request which, in your capacity as good citizens and law-abiding men, you may not grant. I want to tell you, also, that you are condoning no offense against the statutes; that there is not a particle of legal evidence before us of the criminal antecedents of Mr. Charles Byng, except that which has been told you by the innocent lips of his betrothed, which the law of the land has now sealed forever in the mouth of his wife, and that our own actual experience of his acts have been in the main exculpatory of any previous irregularity—if not incompatible with it. Briefly, no judge would charge, no jury convict, on such evidence. When I add that the young girl is of legal age, that there is no evidence of any previous undue influence, but rather of the reverse, on the part of the bridegroom, and that I was content, as a magistrate, to perform the ceremony, I think you will be satisfied to give your promise, for the sake of the bride, and drink a happy life to them both."

I need not say that we did this cheerfully and even extorted from Bill a grunt of satisfaction. The majority of the company, however, who were going with the through coach to Sacramento, then took their leave, and, as we accompanied them to the veranda, we could see that Miss Polly Mullins's trunks were already transferred to the other vehicle under the protecting seals and labels of the all-potent Express Company. Then the whip cracked, the coach rolled away, and the last traces of the adventurous young couple disappeared in the hanging red dust of its wheels.

But Yuba Bill's grim satisfaction at the happy issue of the episode seemed to suffer no abatement. He even exceeded his usual deliberately regulated potations, and, standing comfortably with his back to the center of the now deserted barroom, was more than usually loquacious with the expressman. "You see," he said, in bland reminiscence, "when your old Uncle Bill takes hold of a job like this, he puts it straight through without changin' hosses. Yet thar was a moment, young feller, when I thought I was stompt! It was when we'd made up our mind to make that chap tell the gal fust all what he was! Ef she'd rared or kicked in the traces, or hung back only ez much ez that, we'd hev given him jest five minits' law to get up and get and leave her, and we'd hev toted that gal and her fixin's back to her dad again! But she jest gave a little scream and start, and then went off inter hysterics, right on his buzzum, laughing and cryin' and sayin' that nothin' should part 'em. Gosh! If I didn't think *he* woz more cut up than she about it; a minit it looked as ef *he* didn't allow to marry her arter all, but that passed, and they was married hard and fast—you bet! I reckon he's had enough of stayin' out o' nights to last him, and ef the valley settlements hevn't got hold of a very shining member, at least the foothills hev got shut of one more of the Ramon Martinez gang."

"What's that about the Ramon Martinez gang?" said a quiet potential voice.

Bill turned quickly. It was the voice of the Divisional Superintendent of the Express Company—a man of eccentric determination of character, and one of the few whom the autocratic Bill recognized as an equal—

who had just entered the barroom. His dusty pongee cloak and soft hat indicated that he had that morning arrived on a round of inspection.

"Don't care if I do, Bill," he continued, in response to Bill's invitatory gesture, walking to the bar. "It's a little raw out on the road. Well, what were you saying about Ramon Martinez gang? You haven't come across one of 'em, have you?"

"No," said Bill, with a slight blinking of his eye, as he ostentatiously lifted his glass to the light.

"And you *won't,*" added the superintendent, leisurely sipping his liquor. "For the fact is, the gang is about played out. Not from want of a job now and then, but from the difficulty of disposing of the results of their work. Since the new instructions to the agents to iden- tify and trace all dust and bullion offered to them went into force, you see, they can't get rid of their swag. All the gang are spotted at the offices, and it costs too much for them to pay a fence or a middleman of any standing. Why, all that flaky river gold they took from the Excelsior Company can be identified as easy as if it was stamped with the company's mark. They can't melt it down themselves; they can't get others to do it for them; they can't ship it to the Mint or Assay Offices in Marysville and 'Frisco, for they won't take it with- out our certificate and seals; and *we* don't take any undeclared freight *within* the lines that we've drawn around their beat, except from people and agents known. Why, *you* know that well enough, Jim," he said, suddenly appealing to the expressman, "don't you?"

Possibly the suddenness of the appeal caused the expressman to swallow his liquor the wrong way, for he was overtaken with a fit of coughing, and stammered hastily as he laid down his glass, "Yes—of course—certainly."

"No, sir," resumed the superintendent cheerfully. "They're pretty well played out. And the best proof of it is that they've lately been robbing ordinary passengers' trunks. There was a freight wagon 'held up' near Dow's Flat the other day, and a lot of baggage gone through. I had to go down there to look into it. Darned if they hadn't lifted a lot o' woman's wedding things from that rich couple who got married the other day out at Marysville. Looks as if they were playing it rather low down, don't it? Coming down to hardpan and the bed rock—eh?"

The expressman's face was turned anxiously towards Bill, who, after a hurried gulp of his remaining liquor, still stood staring at the window. Then he slowly drew on one of his large gloves. "Ye didn't," he said, with a slow, drawling, but perfectly distinct, articulation, "happen to know old 'Skinner' Hemmings when you were over there?"

"Yes."

"And his daughter?"

"He hasn't got any."

"A sort o' mild, innocent, guileless child of nature?" persisted Bill, with a yellow face, a deadly calm and Satanic deliberation.

"No. I tell you he *hasn't* any daughter. Old man Hemmings is a confirmed old bachelor. He's too mean to support more than one."

"And you didn't happen to know any o' that gang, did ye?" continued Bill, with infinite protraction.

"Yes. Knew 'em all. There was French Pete, Cherokee Bob, Kanaka Joe, One-eyed Stillson, Softy Brown, Spanish Jack, and two or three Greasers."

"And ye didn't know a man by the name of Charley Byng?"

"No," returned the Superintendent, with a slight suggestion of weariness and a distraught glance towards the door.

"A dark, stylish chap, with shifty black eyes and a curled-up merstache?" continued Bill, with dry, colorless persistence.

"No. Look here, Bill, I'm in a little bit of a hurry—but I suppose you must have your little joke before we part. Now, what is your little game?"

"Wot you mean?" demanded Bill, with sudden brusqueness.

"Mean? Well, old man, you know as well as I do. You're giving me the very description of Ramon Martinez himself, ha! ha! No—Bill! You didn't play me this time. You're mighty spry and clever, but you didn't catch on just then."

He nodded and moved away with a light laugh. Bill turned a stony face to the expressman. Suddenly a gleam of mirth came into his gloomy eyes. He bent over the young man, and said in a hoarse, chuckling whisper:—

"But I got even after all!"

"How?"

"He's tied up to that lying little she-devil, hard and fast!"

To see our other great titles,
visit us at:

BLACKBIRD BOOKS
www.bbirdbooks.com

www.ingramcontent.com/pod-product-compliance
Lightning Source LLC
Chambersburg PA
CBHW030502260626
47157CB00005B/1609